Palm Springs HEAT

Palm Springs HEAT

FAST LANE ROMANCE #1

DC THOME

Palm Springs Heat Fast Lane Romance #1 is a work of fiction. All characters, situations and dialog are products of the author's imagination. Any resemblance to events or to persons, living or dead, is entirely coincidental. Also available for purchase as an ebook from Amazon. com or as a free download for Kindle Prime members. Originally published in 2011 *as Fast Lane by Dave Thome.*

November, 2012 Edition

Published by T2W Inc.

For Mary Jo, my lifelong romance story.

ONE

*T*he limo jerked hard to the right, sending Lara Dixon sliding across the slick leather seat.

That can't be good.

The man seated across from her—the man Gina had found to introduce her to Clay Creighton—scrambled upright and banged on the plexiglas partition separating them from the driver, a uniformed woman who had quarter-inch silver hair peeking from beneath a livery cap.

"What the hell?" he demanded as the partition slid open. "Did you hit something?"

The driver met Lara's questioning gaze in the rear-view mirror. "Oops." The partition slid shut.

That really can't be good.

Lara flipped down a mirror to fix her hair, Her natural color shimmered through the semisweet chocolate veneer. *Hard to get used to after thirty-two years as a blonde.*

"Just a bump in the road." Anton Roche worked his neck like a preening turkey and settled back in as the limo raced past Paradise Cove on the road to Malibu. "As I was saying, the girl thought she was the aurora borealis, Liberty's torch and the leprechaun's pot o' gold rolled into one. But she knew she looked even hotter in my bustier."

Lara suppressed a sigh. *How does Gina put up with this guy?* The lingerie designer had prattled about his life with the glitterati from the minute he'd picked her up at her humble Santa Monica apartment. She wished he'd let her concentrate on this new experience of riding in luxury. After tonight, she might never step into a limo again. Then again, Roche had put his turkey neck on the line to talk up Lara to Clay Creighton.

He has his own axe to grind, but I should at least pretend to be interested.

"Why is it the 'STP' bustier?" Lara asked, though after weeks of researching Creighton's Fast Lane empire, she knew the answer. *Never hurts to practice. You'll be lying all the time if everything goes right tonight.*

Roche straightened with pride. "'Seconds to Paradise.' It's goddamn brilliant. Builds up the bust—and a man can unhook it one-handed like that." He snapped his fingers. "You know how much money Creighton's made from that thing? It's the biggest seller in the Toy Store. But do I get the credit?" He looked more closely at Lara. "It wouldn't have been a bad idea for you to wear one tonight."

Lara had considered buying one from Fast Lane's notorious online gift shop back when she was married. "I thought STP had something to do with gasoline."

"Yeah, well...Fast Lane: Racy cars, the high life... and all that."

Fast women, fast cars, fast living. I know all about Fast Lane and Clay Creighton.

Lara looked out the window as Roche chattered on. The sun drifting down through the maritime haze toward Point Dume reflected in her diamond-blue eyes. The conflagration of red, orange and purple looked no different from here than it did from the bluffs on the other side of Santa Monica Bay.

The limo jerked again as they turned up a gravel road. Lara's heart quickened. *We must be close.*

"We're here!" Roche announced as the car turned into a driveway that twisted skyward through desert terrain. "Are you ready?"

Lara thought about the weeks she'd spent in the gym. The coaching sessions on how to lie with a mysterious woman whose name and accent changed daily. The hours poring through the enormously popular Fast Lane website, reading Creighton's daily encyclicals on materialism and carnality until she could easily extemporize on the advantages of gadgets she'd never use and the attributes of running backs she'd never cheer for.

But everything she learned did nothing to change her opinion: Fast Lane was nothing but a place where men like her asshole ex, Kyle, could leer at naked women and find validation for believing they deserved their own harems.

An instructional guide on how to screw over your wife.

She closed her eyes and her mind to escape Roche's jabber. When she had approached Gina Wray, creator of the pro-woman website HardCoreGrrrls.com, with the idea of infiltrating Fast Lane to reveal its sordid secrets, Lara had never expected to be the one doing the infiltrating.

"I know plenty of people who'd like to bring Clay Creighton down—people who'd pay big bucks for an exposé," Gina had told Lara. "Putting an end to The Rotation wouldn't be so bad, either."

The Rotation consisted of three women who were at Creighton's beck and call 24/7. Every six months, he dumped the most senior member and introduced a new plaything. Relationships arced, he said, starting out passionate and ending up routine, so a man had to bring in "new talent" to keep things exciting. Gina's plan was for Lara to become the first woman in The Rotation's disgraceful sixteen-year history to dump him instead.

"I don't know," Lara had protested. "I'm not exactly Fast Lane material."

"The material is there," Gina had assured her. "You just have to move it around a little."

Nothing's simple. The world is warm and cool and open and mysterious and bright and muddled—all at the same time. How do you live with that?

Lara opened her eyes to see Roche staring at her chest. He frowned. "Can't you show a little more cleavage?"

Lara reflexively looked down the ruffled collar of her dress—a sleeveless midnight blue Roland Mouret crepe Gina had purchased for this night. Lara marveled at how easily the twenty-five-hundred-dollar price tag convinced her the dress fit and felt better than anything she'd ever worn.

But does it look good enough?

Even with her new body and hair, even with every follicle below her forehead sugar-waxed and ripped clean, her nails filed, polished and buffed to a mother-of-pearl sheen, her feet soaked in lavender-scented Dead Sea salt water and tucked neatly into a pair of Guillaume Hinfray platform slingbacks, even after two months of Gina's pep talks, she had to ask this clown, "Do you believe I can even *get into* The Rotation?"

Roche leaned back against the velvety leather, his beady black eyes taking in Lara's slender five-foot-eight-inch frame, long legs, toned and spray-tanned

5

arms. She held steady under his gaze. He reached up and pushed a lock of hair off her forehead. She knocked his hand away and moved the hair back.

"Eh," Roche said. "Stranger things have happened."

Just what I needed: a big boost of confidence.

The limo crested a hillock and slowed to a stop. A busty young woman wearing the lowest-cut Lakers jersey Lara had ever seen opened the door. "Welcome to the ICE House!"

* * *

Clay Creighton moved from his suite of rooms to the portico, where he could look down at the partyers gyrating to a pulsing beat on the massive structure known as the Upper Deck. His trademark white Egyptian cotton shirt hung unbuttoned, and the ocean breeze blew it open to reveal his taut six-pack abs and well-defined chest. His eyes—the irises sparkling like amber in the light of the tiki torches below—scanned the assembled multitude.

"Watching over your subjects, your highness?" The low, sensuous voice of Sun-Li Hwa came from behind Clay. She joined him at the railing, snuggling up against his back and ruffling his dark, wavy hair.

"Yes, my lady," he said, a dry smile forming on his lips. "It does my heart good to see the peasants so happy."

"Am I your lady?"

"One of them."

Sun jabbed him in the kidney.

"Ooh. I like that."

"I wasn't being nice."

"Is there a problem?" Clay turned and looked into her face. He could not help, though, letting his eyes wander down the neckline of her tastefully sequined black Massimo Rebecchi dress that plunged to within an inch of her bellybutton. Her dark olive skin glowed gold in the flickering torchlight.

"I'm not complaining," Sun said.

"Of course you're not. Why would you?"

Someone called to Clay from below. Clay smiled and held up a finger to indicate he'd be down in a minute.

Sun had a mischievous look as she ran her index finger in little curlicues down Clay's chest.

"My subjects need me, my dear," Clay said.

"What about me? I have needs."

"You already have everything you need."

Sun buttoned Clay's shirt. "I don't know what I'm going to miss most."

"I have a feeling you never miss much."

"You've made me feel like a queen."

"You *are* a queen," Clay said. "Now, get the other girls. Our audience awaits."

* * *

The beat pounded louder as Lara and Roche approached the Upper Deck. A bodyguard with an earpiece microphone blocked the entrance, but stepped aside and nodded to Roche.

"That's a good sign," Roche said privately to Lara. "He thinks you're just another one of the unbelievably hot babes who naturally gaggle around me."

"You design lingerie," Lara said, welcoming the banter as an antidote to her mounting nervousness.

"You don't think I do it just for the money?"

Maybe I can work a deal with Gina to murder this guy. Or just do it as a public service.

"Anyway, you blend." Roche did a quick once-over of the ocean of undulating bodies. "On the other hand, the crowd does

seem rather ho-hum. But, like I always say, 'The duller the setting, the more the gem shines.'"

He waded into waves of humanity.

The crowd is ho-hum? Lara tried to convince herself there was even half a chance that was true. The women all had tiny waists, creamy legs and abundant hair. Hips were scarce, but Lara noted collagen-engorged lips and silicone-enhanced upper thoraxes aplenty. And some of the males bobbing around in that gulf stream of prettified people might mature into men sooner or later.

Minnows. I'm after bigger game. A shark, no less. Fully grown and experienced. She had to adopt the mindset of a barracuda. Or maybe a dolphin. Her goal was to disorient the beast with a blow to the belly, then disgorge his ego, thus delivering all of female kind from his predatory ways.

"Hey, weren't you in my chem class?" A morsel of nascent manhood grinned as though he were the first guy ever to think of that sophomoric college line.

"What school?" Lara answered with a tease.

"Pepperdine, duh."

Even from a few feet away, Lara could make out the distinct aroma of man perfume. The kind that's always on sale at the local drugstore.

"What year did you graduate?" she asked.

"Next year."

"Wow. Your parents must be proud." Lara patted his shoulder. "Get back to me when your resume is, um, a little more filled out."

Lara chuckled as she wended her way to the bar. She had never talked to a man that way, for fear of being labeled a bitch. But bitchy felt kind of good. Still, she was relieved to see when she got to the rail that the Pepperdine dude had already located a *chica* who appeared more likely to share some chemistry with him. Lara didn't want to hurt anybody's feelings.

Or, at least, not everyone's.

The server was a brunette stuffed into what was

basically a racecar driver's fire suit cut into pieces held together with black electrical tape, which made her look like an S&M version of Danica Patrick. She nodded to Lara as she mixed a vodka Collins and set it in front of a cutesy blonde.

"I'll have a Karhu," said a hunky schoolboy who clung to Cutesy like a polyester dress. "And give me some head."

The bartender pursed her lips as she poured the beer into a tall glass. "One Finnish lager," she said. "You can suck off the head yourself if you want."

Schoolboy didn't seem to hear. Apparently Lara proved a strong enough distraction to snare his wandering gaze. Cutesy gave her the evil eye.

Lara turned to the bartender and said, "I'll have what she's having."

Two nanoseconds later, Cutesy led Schoolboy away like a dog on a leash.

"Somebody's smoking tonight," the bartender said.

"I haven't even turned on the heat," Lara responded. It felt strange to hear herself talking that way. She noticed that the bartender's nametag said "Danica."

"Um...is your name really...?"

"Weird, isn't it?" the bartender said as she reached under the bar.

"I didn't mean it like that."

"No problem. All the servers get a sport." Lara glanced around and saw a woman in a football getup, another in a hockey uniform and still another dressed like a jockey. Each costume had bondage-style electrical tape alterations similar to the racing suit. "The racing outfit didn't fit anyone else."

She put down a tall Collins glass hand-painted with topless hula dancers swaying beneath palm trees. "Besides," she said, "my name has a K instead of a C. They spelled it wrong on the tag."

Lara laughed. The drink wasn't even made, and she was already more relaxed. Danika was just about to pour rum into a shaker when Lara stopped her.

"On second thought," Lara said, looking Danika straight in the eye, "I'd like a Centurion."

Danika arched one eyebrow. "You're not here just to turn on the heat," she said as she tucked the Collins glass back under the bar and replaced it with what looked like a martini glass crossed with a goblet. "You're here to bring on the sweat."

Lara watched as Danika poured two shots of Crown Royal Extra Rare Heritage Blend into an ice-filled, chrome-plated shaker, chased by a shot of Italian vermouth and a dash of Cynar. After the artichoke-based liqueur entered the mix, Danika gave Lara a knowing look, and then splashed in some more.

"I'm guessing you don't like it too sweet," Danika said as she swizzled the concoction. The resulting amber liquid looked tantalizingly evil as it sloshed into the goblet-cum-martini glass. Finally, Danika dropped in a garnish of orange zest and a maraschino cherry skewered by a tiny, bright green—

"Is that what I think it is?" Lara bent to look more closely at the skewer, shaped like a little man, with the cherry firmly affixed to his not-so-little manhood.

"You didn't want a cherry?" Danika asked.

"Oh, no, it's fine." Lara removed the skewer from the drink and extricated the cherry from the skewer with a click of her incisors.

"Nice." The barkeep attached a cherry to another miniature prong and popped it into Lara's glass. "I've got a feeling that whoever goes home with you tonight's going to end up with a bit more than he can chew."

Suddenly, the music went quiet. All eyes turned toward the steps that descended to the Upper Deck. Clay Creighton himself was already halfway down. With his trademark Centurion in hand, he absolutely basked in the spotlight. Lara's mouth went dry, her heartbeat ticked up a notch. Partly because her moment of truth drew near. But partly because Clay was more handsome in person than in the photos she'd seen on everything from the websites to print magazines and newspapers to late-night paparazzi shows on TV. His dark hair was playfully tousled in front. His square jaw cut a stark profile.

Just beyond his glow, in a glow of their own, came the current denizens of The Rotation: Sun, Taequanda Davis and Corynne McFee.

My god! They're even more gorgeous than I imagined!

Sun, tall and slender, her shiny, jet-black hair bouncing and tickling her bronze shoulders, embodied elegance, like a sexy cigarette ad from the 1950s. Taequanda, more athletic, wore her hair up with spiral curls dangling to her eyebrows. The way she ran her tongue across the purple gloss on her full lips suggested a sexual power greater than Lara had ever perceived in another woman. Corynne had red hair and large eyes that made her look like a girl-next-door type from an old movie. All three stood bolt-straight, struck Miss America poses and smiled dazzlingly.

"Welcome to the ICE House," Clay said, raising his right hand in a gesture of hospitality, "where the good times begin—and never come to an end." He paused for a cheer. "I see you've already discovered that I keep a plentiful stock of the finest libations in the world."

Another cheer. Several partyers raised their drinks.

"And, I think you'll agree I also keep a plentiful stock of the most desirable examples of humankind." The cheering was appreciably louder—and the women were as enthusiastic as the men. "Remember, there is only one rule here at the ICE House."

Let me guess: There are no rules.

"No inhibitions allowed!"

Well, that's different.

Clay raised his glass in a toast as the music ramped back up.

Lara had to admit it was an impressive display. Garish and narcissistic, but impressive nonetheless.

As she sipped her drink, Lara caught a glimpse of Anton Roche oozing toward Clay.

* * *

Clay smiled and nodded his way through the crowd. Playing the part of the jaunty host was one of Fast Lane's Rules of the Road. "The host has to have his head fully in the game, or the event is lost," read rule No. 14. Even so, right now, Clay was faking it. The parties had become tedious. They were just too much alike. The pulsing music. The bobbing throng. Even the abundance of yummy flesh. And yet, Clay was, by his own rules, *required* to look interested. It would be bad business for the world's foremost connoisseur of automobiles, ostentatious living and the human female to show any sign of ennui.

And now, the gauntlet. Women would shake their stuff in his face, attacking him from all angles, hoping to catch his eye with an eye to joining The Rotation. It didn't help that every woman on the deck was well aware that Sun's setting time was approaching.

If only they knew.

He pasted on a smile as he talked to a comely little thing. Or, at least, as she talked and he nodded now and then. He wondered if she could tell he was phoning it in. Oddly, he didn't care as much as he would have just a few years ago.

What's going on with me? Clay found it impossible to focus on the waif's chattering. Something about a movie? *This girl is good-looking enough. Nice rack. Face. Lips. Some hips would be nice.*

He uncharacteristically allowed his eyes to wander, breaking Rule of the Road No. 1: "Make a woman feel like she's the center of the universe."

A familiar face emerged.

"Clay! Great party," Roche effused.

"Anton...thanks. Have you met..." He turned to the comely little thing, expecting her to say her name, but she missed the cue. "Um...this is Anton Roche."

"Cool," she said.

After an awkward pause, Clay said, "Anton invented the top you're wearing."

"Really? I have three. Presents from three different men."

Roche's nod had a distinctly sardonic edge.

"Funny, though," she giggled, "I thought you'd be gayer."

Clay staved off a laugh. *Funny—I thought the same thing. At first.*

"Sorry to disappoint you," Roche said without an ounce of contrition.

The hint flew right past her, so Clay filled in the blank. "Anton and I have some business to discuss."

"Okay, cool," she said, but her mouth continued to engage. Clay watched her lips bob and wondered how anyone could be that self-absorbed.

Clay smiled, patted her on the shoulder and turned away.

Roche put his mouth close to Clay's ear. "The woman I told you about is here."

"Great," Clay answered. There was enthusiasm in his voice, but not in his heart. Sure, he had listened to everything Roche had said about this wonder woman named Lara. But Clay remained skeptical. Someone was always bragging up some woman. But the matchmakers rarely, if ever, got it right. While most women who angled to join The Rotation fully understood it was a business proposition, few understood the process. The process was everything, but it was also a closely guarded corporate secret. Fast Lane thrived on mystique.

"That's her, over by the railing," Roche said, pointing out Lara.

Hmmm...tall. Not Amazon tall; a good height. Classic lines. Slim, but in a healthy way. No obvious signs of collagen or silicone. Definitely works out. Not too cool or pouty or hey-don't-I-look-like-a-model or I-think-I'm-some-kind-of-goddess.

Roche leaned into Clay. "You like?"

"I do." *But why?*

There must be a reason. After all, he was Clay Creighton, and Clay Creighton knew women.

TWO

*G*lancing back, Lara saw Clay moving toward her.

"The view is amazing from here," he said.

Lara continued to focus on the moonlit waves. "Yes, I love the ocean."

"Me, too," Clay said. "But I'm not talking about the ocean."

Clay stepped next to Lara, close enough to feel the heat of her body.

"That's quite a line," she said. "Do you use it often?"

"No, actually, I try never to use a line more than once."

"That must be difficult."

"Oh?"

Lara looked back at the ocean. "I know who you are."

"It's true, I meet lots of women. But I don't use a line on every one of them."

"Because they're always interested?"

"Because I'm *not* always interested."

Oh, this guy is smooth.

"That's not what I've read."

"Then you've been reading lies."

"I've been reading your website."

"Like I said."

Lara looked at him. His smile and that golden sparkle in his eyes. *Easy to see why so many women are interested.* She sipped her drink.

"Roche has been telling me about you," Clay said.

"Nice things?"

"I guess he thought it was up to me to find out the naughty things."

Lara chuckled. "*Another* line? You must really be interested if you're willing to use up two."

"Okay, we can put the naughty things on hold. That still leaves us plenty to talk about."

"Where should we start?"

"How about—"

A coquette who packed way too much under her blouse, considering how little meat hung elsewhere from her bones, put a hand on Clay's shoulder and her mouth close to his ear.

"Hey stud," she said, "wanna go play? I brought toys." She rubbed her "toys" against him.

Clay nodded apologetically to Lara, then turned to face the woman, who had obviously imbibed more than her skinny frame could process, and looked directly into her eyes.

"You are delightful, but I'm already speaking with this other lovely lady right now. So, hold on to that thought, and maybe we can explore it later." He arched an eyebrow to signal for a nearby security man to help the wobbly woman away. Then Clay turned back to Lara.

"Sorry about that."

"You don't have to apologize. I'm sure it happens all the time."

"Welcome to my life."

"Poor baby, always being hounded by women."

"Sarcasm. I like that in a woman."

"I didn't mean to be sarcastic."

"Me either," he said. "Sarcasm is honest. I don't get a lot of that." He turned toward the ocean. "She did have one good idea. We could go somewhere else. Get away from this loud music. All these interruptions."

Oh, my god! The plan's working! And with so many hot, young bodies everywhere. What did Roche tell this guy?

Lara's training clicked in. She wasn't exactly lying. But she absolutely needed to keep cool.

"I didn't bring any 'toys.'"

"I don't know about that," Clay said, his eyes scanning Lara up and down. "I'm not asking you to share them. We could start out just talking. Anton said you know something about race cars."

Clay escorted Lara past the hot tub, crammed with a dozen people who had shed most, if not all, of their clothing, to steps that vanished between huge rocks.

"You're not going to leave your own party?"

"You know about that rule?" Clay beamed. "I have another rule that takes precedence in this case: Never pass up a chance to spend quality time with an alluring lady."

"That's a rule I don't want you to break."

They descended to just above where the waves rammed the cliff and shattered into billions of crackling, foamy bubbles. They crossed a bridge over some jagged rocks and approached two wide glass panels. Clay clicked a button on a key fob and the panels slid apart.

He extended a hand to help Lara up a step. "Welcome to the War Room."

* * *

The War Room had a decidedly retro-lounge feel, about as guy as you could get, with sports memorabilia dominating the décor. *So much stuff.* Footballs signed by the quarterback of every Super Bowl champion. Helmets. Goggles Michael Phelps wore while winning a gold medal at the Olympics. A seat from a classic Porsche. And photos of Clay with star athletes, world leaders and movie stars. Lots and lots of photos. Clay with LeBron. Clay with Venus. With Barack. Stephen Hawking. Vin Diesel.

Clay crossed over to a bar, where he punched a few numbers to make music play from acoustically perfect hidden speakers. "You like Esquivel?"

"Who doesn't?"

"Brandy?"

"Why not?"

"I have Remy and Camus."

"Either one."

Clay held up a heart-shaped bottle. "The Camus comes from a single vineyard from the Borderies district."

"Sounds great." Lara wasn't lying about Esquivel. She associated the avant garde Mexican jazz pianist with her father, who had played his records all the time. Brandy she knew less about.

Clay put two amethyst-colored crystal brandy snifters on the bar and started to pour, but stopped abruptly. "You know what? Let's go with the Remy." He put the stopper back into the Camus bottle, uncer-emoniously tossed out the shot of cognac he'd already poured, then got out a new snifter and a striking decanter that looked liked it was made of quicksilver.

"Louis the Thirteenth," Clay said. "Black Pearl."

Lara could tell from his tone that this was some-thing special. "Black Pearl. Wow," she said, trying to sound knowledgeable.

Clay poured about a shot and a half into each tulip-shaped glass and handed one to Lara. He swirled his, then sniffed it. Lara followed suit, and found it pleasantly aromatic. They pinged glasses and sipped. It tasted velvety and smooth, completely lacking in the throat-clenching bite that years ago had moved Lara to swear off brown-colored liquor.

Not as bad as I thought it would be. "Exceptional," she said.

"There's a story about a Japanese businessman who paid $34,000 for one bottle," Clay said.

"Thirty-four *thousand*?" Lara felt instantly guilty for thinking she might not finish what was in her glass.

"I didn't pay that much," Clay said reassuringly. "Connections."

Lara peered into her glass.

"So, do you like it?" Clay asked.

"Oh, it's great. I mean...Louis the Thirteenth. It doesn't get any better."

"I meant the room."

"Oh." Lara looked around. "It could—"

"—use a woman's touch?"

"If this is the place you bring women when you want to impress them."

"Actually, this is where I go when I don't feel like impressing anyone." He was as creamy and smooth as the ganache in a Lindor truffle. And just as much a threat to the heart. Lara was sure he could make any woman feel he was her destiny.

A temporary destiny.

"So," Lara said, "you're *not* trying to impress me?"

"Do you want me to?"

Lara noted his wry smile. "I guess I should be impressed that you thought to bring me here."

Clay raised his glass to her before taking another sip of cognac.

"*This* is impressive," Lara said as she turned to the seat from the Porsche. "From a 908 Spyder, right?"

"Talk about impressive." He stopped short.

"What?"

Clay pointed to his ear. "The music."

Mucha Muchacha. The marimbas and horns and the interplay of a man's and a woman's voice made Lara nostalgic. She also knew what came next—and sang it out loud.

Clay had the same idea.

They both laughed.

"I've never known any woman who knew *that* song by heart," Clay said. "Or one who could tell me where that car seat came from." He stood shoulder-to-shoulder with Lara and studied the seat. She relished the touch of cotton on her bare arm.

"So, this particular seat," he said, "came from the car that took Targa Florio in '60. The owner gave the seat to my dad, so it's kind of special to me."

Lara perked up. She knew about the annual race through the mountains of Sicily.

"My father was a big racing fan," she said. "He took me with him to races and car shows. When I was eight, he somehow wangled a chance to take a couple of laps at Oxnard in an Austin Healey."

"Those are fast," Clay said.

"I remember the wind blowing through my hair, the grandstand swirling by in a blur."

She remembered more than that. She remembered her father positively glowing through the entire ride. But she also remembered that, as easy as it would have been for him to have become lost in the moment, he had offered to let his little girl move the shifter as he powered down into a turn. Little gestures like that set a standard of behavior toward females that no other man in Lara's life ever met.

"Anyway, I look around and see racing. Football. The *Fast and the Furious* guy," she said. "But I don't see anything related to war."

"Everything's related to war. On some level, at least."

"One tussle after another?"

"One person wants something. Another person wants something else. Or maybe they both want the same thing. So they compete. Do battle. Tussle."

"Two people can't want the same thing and work together to get it?"

"Sure. But there's always going to be a third person who feels left out."

"Somebody wins, somebody loses?" Lara tapped a New England Patriots helmet. "That's what it's all about?"

"Ah, you're a win-win kind of person. More?" He held up the Remy bottle.

"No, I'm good."

Clay poured himself more cognac. A little less than the first time.

"I have this very rare bottle of brandy because I outmaneuvered other people who wanted it just as much. All the guys who signed those footballs over there? They and their teammates got really big rings. Guys on other teams got a pat on the back. The driver of that car won a big trophy at Targa; a bunch of other drivers went home empty-handed."

Lara traced Tom Brady's signature on the Pats helmet. "I'll give you sports and business. But love?"

Christ, I can't believe I said the L-word.

"So you've read my blogs. You want to put that on?" Before Lara could answer, Clay slipped the helmet onto her head.

"It's so big!" She spun it so she was looking through the ear hole. Clay laughed and pulled it off.

Lara combed her fingers through her hair, but one errant lock wouldn't straighten. Clay flicked it into place. Lara's lips curved into a Mona Lisa smile.

"The thing about love," Clay said, "is that everyone wants love to be one big 'happily ever after.'"

Lara thought about how her father had adored her mother, even after she bugged out for good on Lara's seventh birthday. She turned away from Clay. "I don't know about that. But it doesn't have to be a *war*."

"What is war?" Clay grew more animated. "People trying to get what they want. Jockeying for control. Looking to impose their will on someone else. That doesn't happen in relationships?"

Lara turned back around. "Sure, but if they're honest with each other—" A surge of guilt shot through her, as though she had touched an electric fence.

"Forget about war for a minute," Clay continued. "Think about...a football game. Football has willing participants who agree to observe rules and boundaries, and all the various parties are thinking every minute about what they have to do to gain the upper hand. Sometimes you go for the quick strike; other times it's best to go slow and break down the adversary's resistance."

"Whoa! Adversaries? In football and war...but in a relationship? You actually believe two people in a relationship are *adversaries*?"

"You actually don't?"

They were in my sham of a marriage.

"I'm sorry, I don't want this to be a downer," Clay said.

Lara knew her aura always got darker when she thought about her marriage. She could feel it. "No, *I'm* sorry," she said. "This is all very interesting."

"I got carried away," Clay said, touching Lara's hand. "Maybe war's too strong a word. People play games, start playing for keeps. Playing for pride. They try to get around the rules. Hit each other hard. Get nicked up. That's all I'm saying."

"But, in war, there can be only one winner." Lara walked to the open door and listened to the waves. "Or no winner."

"You've heard of Sun Tzu?"

Lara turned around.

Clay started, "Know thy self—"

Lara finished, "Know thy adversary."

Clay walked up to Lara. "A thousand battles..."

"A thousand victories."

"So maybe it's not such a bad thing, thinking about love as war."

Lara held out her glass. "Maybe I would like a little more of this."

Clay smiled and took the glass to the bar. Lara sat on a stool across from him.

"You know," Lara said, "maybe the adversary you're talking about isn't the other person. Maybe it's something the two people are battling in themselves."

Clay put the snifter in front of Lara. "Like what?"

Lara swirled the glass and watched the contents settle. "Whatever's preventing them from loving someone else." She took a sip of cognac without looking at Clay.

Clay pursed his lips and tilted his head. "I never thought of it that way. I might have to rethink everything. Reacquaint myself with old Sun Tzu."

Like the part that says, "Secret operations are essential in war; the army relies upon them to make its every move"?

"Don't do it on my account," Lara said. "You have an image to uphold."

"Yeah—Clay Creighton, manly man among men. The kind of guy who gets a bump, spits on it and hustles his ass back onto the field."

Lara laughed. "Okay, now I believe you're not trying to impress me."

"Tough guys don't impress you?"

Lara drank the rest of the cognac in her glass. *This is actually a lot better than I thought it would be.*

"You know," Clay said, "we don't have to be so serious. It's a big world. We should have plenty to talk about. More?"

Lara put the glass down. "Why not?" she said. "I mean, Black Pearl."

* * *

30

"That's it?" Gina Wray adjusted her cat's-eye glasses and moved papers around to uncover her cigarette lighter. "You spent an entire night with Clay Creighton, and all you did was *talk*?"

"That *was* the plan," Lara retorted. "You said I should leave him wanting more."

From where she sat, Lara could see the intersection of Fairfax and Beverly. The bustle of the crowd contrasted with HardCoreGrrrls, a lean operation with only two employees. After her divorce, Lara had turned to the online community of women whose ex-husbands and lovers had, like Kyle, thought The Rotation made it okay to maintain harems. Though she never went into detail, Gina had clearly been on the frontline of the relationship wars.

"No, no. That's good. It's just, I can't imagine too many women spending a night with Clay Creighton without doing anything more than..." Gina paused to light a cigarette. With her platinum five-point bob, she looked like a femme fatale from a '60s spy flick. "I suppose it would not have been a good idea to have fucked him right there on that big ol' overstuffed couch."

Actually, that would have been a great idea. Just not at that moment.

Clay was so handsome. So charming. So adept at making a woman forget about his repulsive Rotation and testosterone-plagued theorics. Lara had started

31

out pretending to be interested in his globetrotting adventures with the beautiful, the well-heeled and the marvelous. Every woman knows listening to a man's stories is a surefire way to make him believe she cares about him. At some point, though, Clay became truly interesting.

"The brandy was good," Lara said.

"He broke out the Black Pearl," Gina said. "That stuff's got to be for special occasions only."

It could have been the brandy or the lateness of the hour, but at one point Lara had imagined leaning over to kiss Clay and unbutton that immaculate white shirt. Her hands had tingled at the thought of caressing his rock-hard chest. Other things tingled when she imagined him unzipping her dress, pressing her back into the couch cushions and working his way from her neck to her breasts with soft, easy kisses. It seemed so real at the time—and still did. Especially when she pictured Clay over her, shirtless, his golden eyes gazing into her eyes as he unbuckled his belt. She could feel her back arch as he held her wrists beside her head and whispered, "What do you think your next move will be?"

Isn't it obvious? Let me help you get me out of this dress.

"Lara?"

"Mmmm..."

"Lara?"

Lara's nose wrinkled. She smelled smoke. Gina had moved around the desk and stood looking down at her. "I said, 'What do you think your next move will be?'"

"Next move?" Lara tried desperately to get back into the moment—and resented having to. She could see in Gina's mirrored walls a hint of red in her face and neck. She felt a little feverish, too, and down below, a little moist. "Right," Lara said to buy time. "All set up. I'm meeting him for dinner at Rev on Tuesday."

"At *Rev*?" Gina froze with the cigarette an inch from her lips.

"That's good, isn't it?"

"Oh, yeah," Gina said. "That's very good."

* * *

Rev was Clay's newest—and poshest—restaurant. In the heart of the Rodeo Drive shopping district, it epitomized L.A.'s fabled consumerist playground. Clay scanned the street scene from his rooftop terrace. The best of the best cars whizzed by: Ferraris, Bentleys, Maseratis, a Lexus or two. Others decorated the curbs like shiny sculptures.

The beautiful people are coming out to play. That included, of course, women who had the looks to entice the gods away from Olympus, but Clay could think only of Lara. It had been that way since he first saw her three days before. It had been a while since he'd focused on one woman this way.

That she knew so much about what was important to him—sports and cars and such—made her unusual. But what really intrigued him was how Lara had challenged him on his theory of love and war. Clay had always preferred the company of smart women—intelligence was sexy—but few women had ever challenged him to the core. Except Sushma. But with her it was business. With Lara, it was an aphrodisiac.

That had happened with only one other woman, but Clay blocked her from his thoughts as he waited for Lara. He saw her on the big couch in The War Room. He imagined a merger of their bodies so powerful it would bring about a merger of their minds, their souls. The fantasy began with his arm brushing against hers as they admired the seat from the Spyder and proceeded with her turning to him wearing a wicked smile and pushing him onto his back, undoing his belt and pulling his pants to his knees.

Straddling him, she whipped off her dress and whisked it playfully across his chest and face before tossing it over her shoulder. He reached up to fondle her natural breasts through the lacy bra, before she dispatched it to the floor and moved close enough for him to reach one nipple, then the other, with his eager tongue.

He saw them trading places so he could kiss her lightly all over, maintaining this soft-touch approach as he continued southward, teasing her flesh with the waft of his breath until he came to the place between her legs where, to his delight, he would find her already wet.

And then the scene in his mind moved to the Upper Deck, where they would be outside, exposed to the whole world and yet alone in the shroud of the night mist. Lara would lean against the railing, her hair blown by the same ocean breeze that drove the tiki torches into a frenzied demonic dance. Clay could distinctly hear the crackle of flames...a siren calling to him from the rocky shoreline.

"Mr. Creighton?"

"Call me Clay."

"Sir?"

Oh, for the love of—

It was Turnbow, Fast Lane's security chief, on the intercom. Clay went to the control panel by the door and flicked the switch.

"Turnbow?"

"Evening, Mr. C."

"I thought it was your night off."

"Yes, sir. Your guest is arriving. Would you like me to escort her up to The Box?"

"No. I'll be right down."

* * *

Lara looked out the window as the limo Clay had sent moved slowly up Rodeo Drive. *Two limo rides in one week!* This ride, though, was tinged with melancholy. Lara thought about her previous visits to this neighborhood. Like most people who walk this mile without the money to back it up, she had always felt like a rubberneck. An interloper. A tourist in her own hometown. She had grown up in a nice enough neighborhood in the valley, but the valley was nonetheless on the wrong side of the proverbial tracks. Except that the barrier separating Lara's L.A. from here wasn't railroad tracks, but mountains.

During her marriage to Kyle Lobo, a producer of low-budget, straight-to-video actioners like *Death Chase* and *Terror Strike: Bel Air* (which had been shot entirely in Encino), Lara had ventured into the shimmering swimming pool of Beverly Hills on occasion. But with her budget, she was barely able to dip her toes into the water.

The car passed a Catalan eatery that charged sixty-five dollars for a hamburger and fries. It amazed her how many people were accustomed to the high cost of extravagance. The dress she was wearing was extravagant, but Gina hadn't batted an eyelash when they found it at Century City. White cotton with a scoop neck and puffs of pima encircling her waist, it looked like something Gina would buy for herself. And while Lara could tell why it didn't cost $23.95, she also saw no reason it should cost nine hundred dollars. Especially since she was wearing it to a glorified sports bar. On the other hand, it looked great with her new dark hair.

The limo pulled to the curb, and as Lara got out, she found herself looking into the face of a pretty young blonde she knew she'd seen somewhere before. On TV? Singing? The blonde looked Lara over with a steely gaze, a look reserved for serious competitors in the mating game, before turning her head with a flick of her ponytail and marching off with her nose high in the air.

That is a very good sign.

An imposing doorman in a coat with epaulets that made his shoulders look even bigger intercepted Lara as she approached the entrance to Rev.

"Welcome, Miss Dixon," he said in a decidedly unimposing voice. "Mr. Creighton is waiting for you."

"Actually," came Clay's voice from just beyond the doorman, "Mr. Creighton couldn't wait, so he came down to meet you himself."

The doorman stepped back as Clay stepped up. "I see you've already met Chip," Clay said. The doorman nodded politely. "And that's my security man, Turnbow."

Turnbow stood against the building, keeping his eyes peeled. He looked like a bank robber.

Chip opened the door.

"Shall we?" Clay placed his hand in the small of Lara's back. Just that gentle touch sent a zing of electric energy through her body. *Did he feel that, too?*

When they were inside, Turnbow put a hand on Clay's shoulder and tried to speak to him privately, but Lara could hear him just fine.

"I assume you will be going to your box?"

"Actually, I assume we'll go to the main floor."

"I think your guest might enjoy the more intimate atmosphere of The Box." Turnbow nodded at Lara and smiled.

"Why don't we ask her? Lara, would you like to go to my private dining room, or to the main floor and rub elbows with the rabble?"

"I don't expect any special privileges," Lara said, smiling back at Turnbow.

"You know I own the place," Clay said. "That means I can dole out privileges to whomever I please."

"I wouldn't mind hanging out with the rabble."

"That settles it, then," Clay said as he guided Lara toward the elevator.

Chip the doorman threw the door to the street open, and shrieks of pubescent girls filled the vestibule. Turnbow joined Chip in forming a human barricade to let a scruffy young man and his entourage slip inside. Lara recognized him from billboards advertising the upcoming initial installment of the umpteenth series of hunky teen vampire movies. *Not bad looking, but a far cry from what's on the billboards.*

Chip and Turnbow managed to stave off the worshippers and get the door closed, but the shrieks still came through loud and clear.

The young lion slouched and shuffled along amidst his unsavory clique—big dudes with shaved heads and lots of tattoos, and women with fake breasts and tramp stamps who looked like they'd been plucked from an Arkansas trailer park.

"Is that...?" Lara wondered.

"Ah, yes." Clay gave the James Dean wannabe a nod of recognition. "I was told he might be coming tonight. Would you like to meet him?"

Lara gave the pretentious cadre of celebrity handlers the once-over.

"Do they always travel with their own armies?"

"The young ones do—until they discover that most of them are leeches and crooks."

"Oh."

"You know," Clay said, "here's another privilege that comes with ownership."

He led her around a corner to where a guard stood watch over an unassuming door.

"Evening, Mr. C." The guard punched some numbers on a keypad and the unassuming door opened to the most lavishly appointed elevator Lara had ever seen.

THREE

The elevator was lined with richly finished bamboo paneling alternating with floor-to-ceiling mirrors. The ceiling itself was one big mirror.

"Interesting décor," Lara mused when they were safely inside. "I wouldn't have expected you to be so big on Asian themes."

"I'm big on Asian themes?" Clay said as he pressed a button.

"The tiki torches at the party the other night?"

"Oh, right. I like tiki torches," Clay said in a far-away voice. Then he snapped back into the moment. "This was a freight elevator before I took over the building—and it was trashed. I went with bamboo because it was the most environmentally responsible material."

Environmentally responsible? It sounded weird, somehow, to hear him say it, though Lara could recall having read something at the Fast Lane website about sustainable materials. Specifically, materials that were sustainable as well as exotic and expensive. Tree-hugging just for the sake of saving the Earth didn't fit the übermanly metropolitan male.

The door opened to the dining room. To say it was gaudy would be kind. Rev didn't just flirt with tackiness, it made wild love to it. It resembled a sports stadium, with tables on a playing field in the center surrounded by concentric rings of tables on tiers that looked like stands. Diners in the lowest rings even sat in fold-down plastic grandstand seats and ate from retractable trays. A ring of private rooms that mimicked luxury boxes lorded over the entire scene.

So this is what a gazillion dollars buys?

Lara realized Rev went beyond the wildest dreams of Fast Lane's founder, Clay's father, Chase. The magazine flourished during the Swinging Sixties with smartly written articles on politics, business, cars, music, travel—and how to mix drinks, dress right and impress women. There were also pictures of shapely girls in swimsuits, though the swimsuits gradually got smaller, then optional, then disappeared.

Chase Creighton died when his ultralight plane crashed into a cliff near Malibu, leaving Clay in charge at age twenty-three. Clay made no changes until taking Fast Lane exclusively online ten years later. After that, the company expanded into all kinds of moneymaking ventures, including the Toy Store, a resort in Palm Springs and Rev.

Lara stepped out of the elevator and onto Astroturf painted with a giant number 50.

"It's football night," Clay said, as though that explained everything. Lara gave him a blank look. He pointed toward glowing H-shaped neon tubes that dominated opposite ends of the room.

"I thought Rev was all about racing," Lara said.

"Thursday is racing night."

"I suppose you take all this out and put in a racetrack every Thursday." Lara said it with tongue in cheek. She knew what went on at Rev. She just thought it would be best to act as if she didn't.

"That's exactly what we do," Clay said. "My marketing people suggested the name Rev to go with Fast Lane, but I didn't want it to be just about racing, so Sushma came up with the idea of changing the décor from one night to the next." Lara recognized the name of Sushma Vishnuveda, a former Rotation member who had risen quickly in the past few years to the highest echelons of the Fast Lane empire. "We can do basketball, baseball, hockey—"

"Hockey? Do the waiters have to skate?"

"That *would* be fun," Clay laughed, "but no, we put down acetate sheets that look more like ice than

43

real ice does. I know that sounds unbelievable, but it really does."

"Do you have a synchronized swimming night?"

"I'm not sure that would appeal to the demo."

Lara scanned "the demo." Every table was occupied. She thought she recognized a face or two. Movie stars. Athletes. At

least one cable news anchor. She could see into the boxes whose giant smoked-glass panels were open and revealed the private parties inside. But no matter where they sat, people seemed to be enjoying themselves.

The people especially seemed to enjoy sneaking peeks at Lara and Clay as they walked across the floor. Lara struggled to look comfortable in spite of her mounting self-consciousness, but something must have tipped off Clay.

"Maybe you'd rather go to my personal box after all," he said.

It might be easier. Then again, she didn't want to make things *too* easy.

"We can stay down here," she said.

"Great," Clay said as they came to the last empty table, under one of the neon goalposts. Clay pulled out a chair for her. "So, is this what you thought the illustrious Rev would be like?"

"I'd heard it was so..."

"Opulent?"

"Yeah."

"Ritzy? Swank? Classy?" He pronounced "classy" as "cuh-lassie," as though it had three syllables.

"Classy sounds right."

"Tell me what you're really thinking." His eyes so gleamed and his face looked so sincere that it was easy to believe he meant it."

"I'm thinking it's unbelievably tacky." Lara stopped. "Ooh. That was a little direct."

Clay laughed. "I like direct. Besides, this place *is* tacky. So tacky, it's cool."

"But all these people. They're so..." Her voice tapered away.

"They're so what?"

"Rich. And famous. And successful."

"And, what? You think just because they're rich and famous they have good taste?"

Lara laughed, which brought a satisfied smile to Clay's face as a waitress wearing a tight-fitting, low-cut referee's jersey and hot pants came to the table.

"Are you ready, Miss Dixon? Mr. C?"

"Oh, but I haven't even seen a menu."

"Menu?" The waitress looked to Clay for an explanation.

"We'll both just have the special," he said. Lara agreed with a shrug. The waitress turned and snapped her fingers, and a guy dressed as a stadium beer vendor lugged over a cooler full of classic-recipe Schlitz and lager glasses on ice. He popped the tops of two bottles and then, holding them by their necks in one hand, simultaneously emptied them into two glasses he held in the other.

"Wow," Lara said, impressed.

She and Clay clinked glasses. As they sipped their beers, a short, Rubenesque biker-leather-clad woman of forty-five with big 1980s-style orange-red hair, no neck and a twenty-two-year-old emo boy with pierced eyebrows and cheeks in tow approached the table.

"Hey, C," the redhead said.

"Lucretia!" Clay started to get up.

"Don't get up on my account," the redhead protested. She turned to the guy. "Muggs, do *you* want him to stand?"

Muggs shrugged and shook his head so that more of his jet-black hair flopped into his face. Clay sat back down. "Lara," he said, "this is—"

"Lucretia Moray," Lara said. "You're on my iPod."

It was true, though just barely. Lara had exactly one of Lucretia Moray's noisy, obscenity-laced songs.

"I have some new shit coming out in a month. No fuckin' ballads this time. Just balls-on rock 'n' roll."

Lara didn't fully hear what Lucretia said. She was preoccupied with Clay, who seemed to be making a cutting-off motion with his fingers right at the bottom of his nose.

"Um...great," Lara said, hoping that was the correct response.

"Anyway, C, we just wanted to come over and check out your...um...date? Nice meeting you, Laura."

"Lara," Muggs said.

"What?"

"Her name's *Lara*, not *Laura*. God!" Muggs sounded irritated—and way too much like Napoleon Dynamite.

Lucretia did not look amused. "You can kiss my enormously fat, ghost-white ass," she said. She flicked even more of Muggs' hair into his face, then turned to Lara and said, "They can be such children."

And with that, she trundled off with Muggs shuffling behind.

"That was weird," Lara said.

"Um..." Clay used his napkin to wipe foam from Lara's lip.

"Oh, no...did I...the whole time?"

"I wouldn't let it bother you. How embarrassed can you be about something like that when you're talking to a woman who's wearing assless chaps with nothing underneath but a leather thong?"

"What?" Lara looked across the room to where Lucretia waited for the elevator, covered chin to toe in black—except for significant portions of her considerable snow-white butt cheeks outlined by shiny rings of burnished steel studs.

Lara's mouth dropped open. "I guess I take that back about the rich and the famous having better taste than everyone else."

Clay laughed hard. A good-natured laugh. "You already knew that," he said. "You had to if you were married to a movie producer for seven years."

"Oh, you checked me out."

"I Googled you." Clay shrugged. "Actually, one of my people Googled you."

"My ex-husband didn't exactly make the kind of movies that would appeal to Meryl Streep," Lara said. "He churned out straight-to-DVD atrocities starring actors who weren't talented enough to do porn."

"Sure. Lobo Rojo Productions. *Savage Sisters of Simi Valley*."

"You've heard of *Savage Sisters of Simi Valley*?" Kyle's stupid movies all employed the same formula: Mix guns and scantily clad women and shake well. Especially the women.

"Seen it six times."

"*Six* times?"

"Give or take."

"All the way through?"

"You have to watch it all the way through. The rampage at the Mulholland Drive mansion where Maura Chesterton and the nuns are keeping the garbage man as their sex slave is classic trash cinema—but if you don't see the opening, it doesn't make much sense."

Lara was stunned. "It doesn't make much sense with or without the opening. Nothing in the movie makes *any* sense."

"Illustrates my point," Clay continued. "Just because you have a million dollars, or a billion, doesn't mean you have good taste."

"I didn't mean to insult you."

"Don't worry." Clay touched her hand reassuringly. "I've been insulted so much, I'm immune. People like what they like. That's all."

People like what they like. Did this come from a deeper measure of wisdom than Lara expected? Or a deeper pile of bullshit? This self-effacing side of Clay—the regular guy who gladly poked fun at his fondness for stupid movies—had not shown itself as she prepared for her mission. *Is he messing with my head?* She had to remember why she was here.

"I was tangentially involved in the business of making movies," Lara said, "but it didn't make me rich or famous. I never even got to hang around with anyone famous."

"Maura Chesterton."

"Anyone who *deserved* to be famous."

Clay laughed. "But hey...you're doing it right now. From right here I can see two Oscar nominees. A Pulitzer-winning novelist. A former ambassador to the U.N." He nodded in the direction of a stubby man with a bad comb-over a few tables away. "Just people.

49

People who have problems and disappointments and bad taste. I could give them elegance, but they come here to let their hair down and act silly. This place is a guilty pleasure for people who need to kick back and blow off steam, just like everyone else."

Lara looked around again. Thinking in Clay's terms made it easier to see just people.

The waitress returned, and Lara couldn't believe what she deposited in front of them: Paper-lined deli baskets holding a hot dog in a bun, some potato chips and a pickle.

"*This* is the special?" Lara said, trying to remain open-minded.

"Actually," Clay said, "it's the only thing on the menu tonight."

"Condiments?" The waitress plunked down a cardboard six-pack container of bottles filled with raw and sautéed onions, sweet relish, mustard, ketchup and an exotic-looking reddish-brown puree.

"Try some of this one," Clay said, pointing to the puree. "It's called 'Secret Stadium Sauce,' and you can only get it in Milwaukee. The Brewers' owner's from here, so I asked him to ship a batch just for tonight."

He practically drowned his sausage in the stuff, then held the bottle out to Lara.

"Really," he said. "It's out of this world."

* * *

When they were done with dinner—dessert was Stephen Colbert's AmeriCone Dream ice cream served in a miniature football helmet—Clay led Lara on a tour. It began in the kitchen, where the well-paid staff of experienced chefs seemed to be enjoying themselves in preparing dinners that sports teams pay teenagers and retirees minimum wage to assemble.

"Is it always so much fun working here?" Lara remarked.

"Yes—and why not?" the head chef said in an accent that could have been French or Greek—Lara couldn't tell. "It is a great honor to be involved with such a noble cause."

Noble cause?

"You didn't know?" Clay asked. "All the money we take in tonight goes to charity."

Lara felt her face getting red.

"It's understandable," Clay went on, acting more embarrassed than Lara felt. "It was an invitation-only event."

"Duh," Lara blurted. "A hot dog and chips? What kind of dope would think…"

Clay laughed a laughing-with-you, not-at-you laugh. "Yes, that would be crazy," he said. "Don't be embarrassed. It's my fault. I should have said something."

"I've heard about this place—everyone has—but I don't remember anything about charity."

"We don't really make a big deal out of it. Don't want to make it look like we're patting ourselves on the back."

A terrible thought struck Lara: What if Clay Creighton wasn't as bad as she had built him up to be? Environmentally responsible bamboo in the elevator. Elaborate dinners for charity. And her

creeping suspicion that he really was interested in her and not just faking it in the hope of scoring. Although she certainly wouldn't mind if he *was* just trying to score.

But, damn it, why can't people just be what they appear to be?

The tour ended in Clay's "personal box," which could have held its own against the most opulent luxury suites in the new Yankee Stadium.

"People come here to watch TV?" Lara stared at the two gigantic high-definition TV screens hanging from the ceiling at opposite ends of the suite.

Clay handed her a glass of deep red wine. "I host game parties. People expect a big screen." He clicked a remote control and bossa nova played from speakers hidden behind the most lavishly stocked bar Lara had ever seen. A few bottles were arranged on a tray on the bar—the ingredients of a Centurion cocktail. Lara picked up the Fast Lane-label Cynar bottle, but put it back down when she realized how obviously phallic it was.

Clay fine-tuned the stereo, tweaking the treble, then the bass, then the treble again. Lara admired his shoulders. *Good angle.*

Lara quickly looked away when Clay turned around. "You like the seats?" he said.

Lara hadn't even noticed she was brushing one of the spectator seats with the back of a hand. "It's so soft," she said.

"Feels like kid leather, doesn't it?"

Oh-oh: Another revelation on the way. No doubt the Clay Creighton that Lara had constructed would install politically incorrect leather seats in his luxury box. But this "new" Clay Creighton?

"It's Alcantara. Man-made. Feels great—cleans up easy," Clay said as he moved close to Lara. "Pretty important when you consider how crazy things can get. Go ahead, spill your wine on the chair. It's like a miracle fabric."

"That's okay. I'll take your word for it."

Lara sipped the wine. It tasted funny. Funny, as in the way good wine tastes to someone who usually drinks the $3.99-a-bottle stuff from the discount bin at Rite-Aid.

"Oh!" she exclaimed, and worried that she sounded surprised, like a rube who didn't know Beaujolais from Hawaiian Punch.

"That tartness at the back of the mouth, it does goose you a little," Clay said.

So it's not just me.

The music caught Lara's attention. *Corcovado.* Lara had a soft spot for the song. It reminded her of warm, carefree summer nights in her childhood. The sun setting over the San Gabriels. Music drifting through the screen door. Her father resting on the porch steps as she colored on the sidewalk with chalk.

Lara became aware of Clay looking at her. How long had he been doing that? And what had he been thinking while her mind was wandering?

"The music," she said.

"I thought you'd like it."

"Why?"

"I don't know."

Clay put down his wine and cozied up to her from behind. Lara closed her eyes as his cheek—freshly shaved—brushed against hers. Clay's cologne smelled as good as the wine: A balanced bouquet, outdoorsy with a hint of spice. Astrud Gilberto's dreamy monotone floated through the air with words about starry nights and windows with views of the mountains and sea.

All evening long Clay had subtly tapped wedges of doubt into chinks of Lara's iron-clad reason. Now he worked on her body as well, stroking her sides from the tops of her hips to just under her arms, allowing his fingertips to venture teasingly past her breasts.

Her whole body flushed with warmth. Every muscle relaxed. Her resistance dissipated in the silky dusk of the dimmed lights. The languor of the tropical music. The welcome pressure of Clay's chest against her back.

It's too soon for this.

And then Lara spilled her wine. A deep purple stain spread over the virgin skin of a seat cushion.

"Fuck!" Lara clamped her hand over her mouth. "I'm sorry!" She felt dumb, but as she grabbed a napkin and daubed furiously, she was thankful for the diversion. *Damn it, Lara, stay focused on why you're here!*

Clay took her hand with the crumpled-up napkin still in it. "You don't have to worry about that." He raised Lara's hand to his lips and kissed her wrist. "Besides, spilled wine is sort of romantic, don't you think?"

He looked at Lara with those glittering golden eyes, then kissed her mouth. Fireworks blew away the quiet nights of quiet stars. *Stay strong.*

"I guess I overreacted," she said when their lips finally parted. "The F-bomb, and all."

"The F-bomb?" Clay laughed. "That's what's bothering you? I haven't had anyone apologize to me for *that* in god knows how long."

He moved toward Lara again. She pulled back. "What about all those people!" She motioned toward the still-crowded dining room.

"They can't see us." Clay stood, moved up close to the window and tapped on the glass. Two couples in grandstand seats nearby looked around for the source of the sound, obviously unable to locate it. For good measure, Clay made a funny face and flipped off the unsuspecting diners with a very assertive double bird.

"See? Nada. You want to try?"

Lara was laughing. "I—I can't."

"Sure you can!" He put his hands on Lara's shoulders and tugged her into position. "Let the F-bombs fly!"

Clay flipped off the couples again. "Hey, you people! F-bomb you! Come on."

Lara couldn't muster even one extended middle finger, let alone two.

"Feels good, doesn't it?" Clay said. "Hey, F-bomb you, Will Railling."

The cable news blowhard? "That's not really—?"

"I don't think so. But he looks just like him."

"He does!"

"Hey, Will, you fatuous bastard." Clay danced around with both badfingers wagging.

Lara laughed so hard she fell back into a seat. Clay plopped into the seat next to her. The one Lara had spilled on.

"Watch out!" she said. "You don't want to ruin that nice white shirt."

"Yeah. I only have thirty-seven more just like it." He rubbed the spill with his back. Then he looked at her with eyes that crackled with light, like sparklers on the Fourth of July. He moved a tendril of hair off Lara's forehead. Lara subtly nodded to make it fall back.

"You're even more beautiful close up," Clay said.

Lara could feel her will melting again. "You—"

"Shhh." Clay put a finger to Lara's lips. "Don't change the subject. We were talking about you."

He ran his fingers down the length of her hair where it had fallen over her shoulder. Then he playfully tugged on one of the little cotton puff balls.

"This is a nice dress," he said. "It looks good with your hair."

"You like dark hair?"

"Sure," Clay responded. "On you."

Another line? Lara shot him a look.

"In general, I like hair on a woman. It's not necessary. But if it's there, then dark, light. Whatever."

"Thank you. I think." Lara's smile contained an ounce of mischief.

Clay smiled. "I'm going too fast, aren't I?"

"I don't mean to—"

"No, it's just that—and this is not going to sound good no matter how I say it—women usually throw themselves at me."

"You're right. There's no good way to put that."

"I'm not saying I'm some kind of superhuman love machine."

Lara laughed.

"It's like an occupational hazard."

Lara laughed harder.

"Women think they can impress me by—"

Lara put her hand on top of his. "Stop! You're digging yourself in deeper."

Clay let out a little laugh, too.

"I had a great time tonight," Lara said. "We could get together again soon. The weekend, maybe?"

"Yeah. I like that idea."

They got up and headed for the door.

"Are you *sure* those people can't see us?" Lara asked, looking back over her shoulder.

"Ninety-nine percent."

Lara flipped off the dining room.

"Hey, that *does* feel kind of good."

* * *

Lara felt in control again by the time she and Clay got back to the elevator. But her mind wandered. In her reverie, he knelt in front of her. She was wedged into a corner. Naked from the waist down. Fingertips digging into the bamboo strips on the wall. Moving subtly to guide Clay's tongue to the sweetest spot. And watching from multiple vantage points in the mirrored panels.

Lara had been on movie sets when such scenes were being filmed, and she'd always thought it would be exciting to be on camera that way. Not R-rated Hollywood style, with sheets obscuring the best parts of the action, but in triple-X mode. Or maybe a home-made sex tape. She wouldn't actually want anyone to see it, but the thought of other people seeing it aroused her.

"Penny for your thoughts," Clay said.

Lara blinked. Clay leaned safely against the opposite wall, but she saw him everywhere in the mirrors.

"Oh, nothing. It's been a long day."

The door opened to Chip's smiling face. "Your car is waiting, Miss Dixon."

When Clay opened the car door for Lara, she glimpsed the stain on the back of his shirt and rubbed it. "I still say it's a shame about the shirt."

"Here," Clay said as he undid the buttons. "It's yours."

What?

"Besides, it's cooler than when you got here." Clay draped the shirt over Lara's shoulders. It was the softest cotton Lara had ever felt.

"I guess I should say thank you," she said.

"The shirt's messed up, so I wouldn't hold it against you if you didn't."

Lara reached up and touched his bare chest. His skin was as smooth as the shirt, but the muscles beneath his skin were firm. *I wouldn't mind if you held this against me.*

Their eyes met. They kissed. Then she got into the car.

She rolled the window down, and the last things she saw as the car moved into traffic were Clay's gleaming irises. Lara put her head back on the overstuffed seat, closed her eyes, and let images of the evening ping through her mind.

FOUR

*A*fter Lara left, Clay could have stayed at Rev to hobnob with the glitterati. He had planned on spending the night in his penthouse above the restaurant, but felt that time breezing down the PCH in his '29 Bugatti would clear his head. Specifically, he had to clear his head of an image that struck him while he leaned against the wall of the elevator at Rev, trying to look cool. He had found himself lost in a fantasy in which Lara stood tucked into a corner, naked from the waist down, fingertips digging into the bamboo strips on the wall, arching her back to guide his tongue to the sweetest spot. And in his mind, he looked up and caught her watching him from the multiple vantage points provided by the mirrored panels.

Now, as he, shirtless again, watched the moon from the railing of the Upper Deck, Sun tickled his back with her perfectly manicured nails.

"Hey," she said. She let the front of her wrap drop open and pressed against Clay.

"Is that how you're supposed to wear that outfit?"

"I could take it off if you don't like it." She blew into his ear.

She was so tall. So slender. So rapturously beautiful. The jet-black hair cascading down her back caught the moonlight in silky undulations.

"You know, you're beautiful in about a million ways," Clay said.

"But, apparently, not in the way that counts most."

One of Clay's eyebrows went up.

"Oh, yes," Sun said, brushing the hair on his chest, "a girl starts to get the hint after eighteen months."

"Don't take it personally."

"I know. We have a business arrangement."

Clay stared out at the black water. "You know who was president when I was your age? Bush. George H.W. The first one."

"You prefer something with a few more clicks on the odometer."

I hate this part. Despite what Clay wrote in his blog, regardless of what his "rules" required, letting go of a woman with whom he had shared so many experiences was more difficult than anyone knew. He always hoped the women would be good sports about it—and they all had been so far. *Well, there was that one.* In a way, Clay had loved all of the women who had passed through The Rotation over the past sixteen years.

"It's that obvious?"

"It's that obvious." Sun shook her head. "Men. You think you're so hard. So inscrutable. But, down deep, you all have soft, mushy centers." She put her wrap back on. "I don't know what's going to become of you, Mr. Mush, Clay Creighton, but I think it'll be interesting to watch."

* * *

"Are you fucking out of your mind?" Sushma Vishnuveda shrieked.

Clay couldn't blame her. People outside her office had stopped to rubberneck, so Sushma shut the door hard to convey more than a hint of authority.

Everything about Sushma's office conveyed more than a hint of authority. It was spartan in the extreme—from the commanding view of the stark crags outside to the interior color scheme, limited to black, silver and tones of gray. An outsized oil painting, a severe study in amorphous gray shapes, tyrannized the room. A black-as-night laminated desk glistened with a funereal quality, and two chrome-and-black-leather chairs in front of it could have been standard issue for an interrogation room. A wide-screen monitor hung from one corner; the desk top held only a wireless mouse, a monitor and a black ceramic teapot on a wooden tray.

Sushma sat on the edge of her desk and towered over Clay. "Bringing this woman to Rev was very unwise. That horrible Lucretia Moray has it all over her Facebook page. You have a brand to protect."

Sushma didn't appear at all imposing. Born to a privileged family in Mumbai, she stood barely five feet tall. But with her fully fleshed-out curves, there was a whole lot of sexy packed onto her frame. She had dark olive skin and a heart-shaped face dominated by round eyes with long lashes that made her look like Bambi when she blinked.

But now Clay was locked in on her scowl. Sushma was not Hindu, but she came on like the deity Shiva—a force that could be creative or destructive, depending on the situation. Her outspoken nature had put her at odds with many in the organization, but because Fast Lane thrived like never before under her command, Clay deferred to her on all business matters.

Being a brand is a pain in the ass.

"So," he said, "the fact that I know Lucretia Moray's no problem, but bringing a guest to my own restaurant is over the line."

"You may bring in your guests. If they are approved. The media have been calling all day to inquire about 'the mystery woman.'"

"It's different with Lara. Maybe..." He pursed his

lips for a moment. "Maybe it's time to think about ending The Rotation."

"My god. Has she stolen your mind?" Sushma leaned until her face was inches from Clay's. "Let me spell it out for you: The restaurants, the resorts, the clothes, the music downloads, the books, the golf clubs, the lingerie—even that godawful brussels sprout liqueur—what do you think happens to all that if you end The Rotation?"

"Cynar is made from artichokes, not brussels sprouts."

Sushma was not amused. Chastened by her icy gaze, Clay continued. "You really believe ending The Rotation will make everything come crashing down? Isn't that why we introduced all this other stuff—so we wouldn't have to rely just on the website for income?"

"The Rotation is not just some abstract notion. It is not some...gimmick. People equate Fast Lane with The Rotation."

"And me."

"Yes...and you. Do you think there is no other place where one can find an article by Neil DeGrasse Tyson? Or a titty shot of some French actress?" She shook her head and muttered to herself like an angry parent, only in Hindi.

"You know," Clay said, "I'm actually the boss here. I think I should have a say in some of these decisions."

"Certainly you own the final say. I am just a hired

gun. You can do whatever you want. But maybe what you want would be more productive if you started thinking with this head"— she poked his temple— "instead of this one." She punctuated her point with a flick of her fingers to Clay's crotch.

"I've been okay so far doing it the other way. Why change now?"

"Because now your little head has given you a truly stupid idea."

Clay could not help but smile, which only infuriated Sushma even more.

"That pushiness," he said. "It's why *you* spent less time in The Rotation than any other woman."

"But one."

"Yes, but one."

"My pushiness, as you refer to it, also happens to be the reason this company still exists."

"So what should I do, Signora Consigliere?"

Sushma rolled her eyes, plunked down into her cushy chair, pressed her hands together and pointed them at Clay as she leaned toward him on her elbows.

Ah, the scrunched-up shoulders. Here it comes.

"This is what I believe we should do," she said. "Bring this Lara Dixon into The Rotation and see how things play out. If you still feel the same about her a few months from now, maybe we can find a way to work it into the grand scheme of things. It is perhaps possible that the great ladies' man, Clay Creighton, has finally

66

decided to settle down with just one woman. Perhaps that will even attract a new audience. But such a move must be thoroughly planned."

"I suppose you're right," Clay said with more than a hint of resignation.

Sushma dialed back the aggression—and even managed to crack half a smile. "Of course I am right. Is that not what you pay me to be?"

Clay shrugged.

"I'm not sure it's what Lara would want," he said. "But I'll give it a try."

* * *

As soon as Clay left, Sushma got on the phone.

Turnbow answered. "Yes, Ms. V?"

"Perhaps you can explain to me what the fuck happened at Rev last evening."

"Ma'am?"

"Do not play dumb with me."

"Bergmann called me as soon as he got word about Mr. C's guest."

"So you knew in advance."

"Yes, but not much. I had to hustle to get down there in time."

Sushma's eyes narrowed. "Why was I not told?"

"I thought I could handle it."

"Afterward."

"Mr. C specifically asked me not to tell you."

Sushma ground her teeth. The look on her face said she wanted to rip out someone's throat. Most likely Turnbow's. Or Clay's. She composed herself by straightening her blouse and patting her hair. "All right, then," she said in a calm, but dangerous, voice, "now *I* am telling you to find out everything there is to know about this Lara Dixon."

"I'll have my people start the usual check as soon as possible."

"I suggest you start sooner than that. By my clock, you have already missed the deadline by, oh, twelve hours."

She hung up the phone by flinging it against the wall.

* * *

Meanwhile, a zillion miles away from Malibu, in the tiny, hot Fairfax district offices of HardCoreGrrrls. com, Gina fiddled with her chrome lighter and laughed. "I'd say you're better at this game than you might think," she said.

"It's not like it's easy," Lara replied.

"Yeah, but he gave you his shirt. His *wine-stained* shirt."

"That is kind of a romantic gesture."

"Fucking molten hot lava romantic." Gina lit a

cigarette, inhaled deeply and held the smoke for a long time. "Clay Creighton's turning out to be every bit the cool, charming bastard everyone says he is."

"You don't think he meant it?"

"Meant it how? Like how he wants to fuck your brains out?"

To put it delicately. "I suppose," Lara said, "I thought it would be good to play it cool."

"Oh, it was. Always leave them wanting more. So what's next?" Gina carefully sculpted the ash of her cigarette, twisting it slowly on the edge of the translucent amber ashtray on her desk.

"I'm not sure. He said he'd call me this weekend."

"You've got clothes for whatever?"

"There's the lemon yellow dress."

"With the white stripes and the..." Gina slashed the air with her cigarette-holding hand to indicate a V neck. "Good. For daytime. What about the evening?"

"I think I'm set, no matter what," Lara said.

"Maybe it's a good time to unleash the crimson dress," Gina said with a naughty grin.

Lara loved the crimson taffeta shift. It screamed flaming hot sex. She had never owned one that color before, and when she tried it on, she got a kick out of looking into a mirror and seeing a Woman in Red. The yellow dress was pretty, like something the nice girl next door would wear on a '60s TV show. But the crimson dress? That one was right out of *Mad Men*.

69

"We'll see," Lara said.

"Okay, then. Keep me up to date."

Lara got up to leave.

"And keep doing whatever it is you've been doing," Gina continued. "You seem to be on to something."

Lara paused. "I've never been good at playing hard-to-get."

"What, you were voted Class Slut in your high school yearbook?"

"I just don't want to, you know, push it too far. I don't want him to lose interest."

"I wouldn't worry about that," Gina said as she ground out her smoke. "I don't get the idea Clay Creighton is the kind of man who easily gives up on things he really, really wants. And he seems to really, really want you."

* * *

On a glorious Saturday morning, Lara sat with a cup of strong coffee on her postage-stamp-size back porch wearing an oversize T-shirt and men's boxers that served as her pajamas. She rested her laptop on her knees and revisited the history of The Rotation. Since it began sixteen years earlier, The Rotation had had thirty-eight members. The average time it took to cycle through was fifteen months, though a woman named Virginia Warren lasted only six weeks. The website gave no hint as to why the woman with the pointy, little chin, smiling innocently from behind a tangle of lemony curls, left so soon.

Sushma's stint in The Rotation lasted seven months.

Lara could not find an explanation of how Clay decided who was in. *He can't just seduce a new dupe and boot an old one out the door.* She felt bad for Sun—and for every other woman who had passed through The Rotation. Then again, there was no guarantee Lara would replace Sun. *Should I play hard to get? Throw myself at him? What turns him on?*

The thought of being intimate with Clay Creighton—*the* Clay Creighton—had appeal. Hell, the thought of being intimate with *any* man seemed like a great idea. Lara had been celibate since the day she came home early from a business trip to San Francisco, where she'd spoken with investors in one of Kyle's inane movies, to the sound of the spa bubbling away. Hot and tired from the grueling drive, Lara decided to launch a sneak naval attack on Kyle. The brutal schedule of completing his latest flick had kept them apart—or so he had led Lara to believe. She came out onto the deck wearing nothing but her high hopes of a foamy frolic, only to discover two other women already living her fantasy.

Two years had passed, but Lara was still haunted

by her response. She had gasped, turned red and dashed out of sight. She had thrown on some clothes and was on her way out the door when it dawned on her that something was missing. Groveling. Lara had peeked through the blinds, expecting at least to find the sluts no longer there. On the contrary. Lara's brief appearance seemed to have been completely inconsequential. That added insult to the injury of having believed Kyle would be content to look at, but not touch, the floozies he worked with every day.

Humiliated, she had left, vowing to get even during the upcoming legal proceedings. But Kyle had no money. Worse, he had racked up big balances on their credit cards spending on other women. *Seven years of marriage and eight years of free labor as a promotions director, and all I got was this lousy car.*

That's when Lara resolved to make ending Clay's cruel farce her personal crusade.

Then, how to eliminate the tingle between her legs every time she thought of him? Lara unconsciously traced her fingers along the boxers' fly as she read a blog entry about the proper way for a man to use his fingers to bring a woman "to completion." That's what Clay's blog said. Not orgasm. Not pleasure. Not climax. Completion. Because without a man, a woman could never be complete—another pillar of the Fast Lane philosophy.

Lara thought for a moment about going inside to her bed to "complete" herself. But no one could see her out here. She couldn't even see the sky without standing at one end of the porch and craning her neck. Towels hung out to dry six months before obscured the view of the apartment behind hers. She had rarely seen whoever lived there outside—and never in the morning. She slipped one hand under the elastic of the boxers; the other snuck up under the tee. *Clay's touch.* She licked her lips. *Clay's kiss.* She reclined in the chair. *Clay's body pushing into mine.*

And then her phone rang.

Fuck!

Lara grudgingly straightened herself up on the chair and checked the caller ID. Clay. *At nine-thirty a.m.?*

"Clay...hi!"

"Hope it's not too early to call."

"No! I was just...working on something."

"Great. I have to run an errand this afternoon, and I was hoping you'd come with me."

* * *

A few minutes before two that afternoon, Lara sat at a table on the terrace at Gardain. Pronounced "jzar-dah," it was a hipster restaurant overlooking Hollywood from a perch between Runyon Canyon and Wattle's Garden Park. Business was brisk, and though the yellow dress didn't match the thrift-store-chic tastes of the calculated bohemian clientele, Lara wasn't worried. She didn't have to impress anyone but Clay.

She'd ordered an appetizer made with giant Japanese tiger shrimp marinated in El Jimador aged tequila and trimmed with an exotic coriander-based garnish containing Black Krim and White Wonder tomatoes. Sure, it cost $42.50—but when would Lara get another chance?

Clay had offered to pick her up at her apartment, but Lara didn't want him to see where she lived. Her Santa Monica neighborhood was a lot nicer than where she'd grown up. But it wasn't the kind of nice that Clay was used to. Lara lied about having to be in Hollywood at midday, so Clay suggested they meet at Gardain because of its "unpretentious menu and modest ambience."

Clay arrived at 2:01, just as the waitress brought the shrimp cocktail to the table.

"Ah, the Black and White Tiger," Clay said without missing a beat. "Very good choice."

The sound of his voice and the sight of those eyes radiating gold in the midday sun made that tingling sensation return. *Maybe this would be a good day to take things to a new level.*

"So, what is this errand?"

"You're just going to have to wait for it. But, feel free to let your imagination run wild until the time comes."

If you say...

Lara speared a shrimp and popped it into her mouth.

FIVE

When they were done eating, Clay led Lara to a parking lot tucked into the hillside behind the restaurant. It featured all the usual vehicular suspects—Mercedes, Audis, a Fisker Karma, more than a few politically incorrect SUVs—but Clay charged past them all to a little '57 Austin Healey "Frogeye" Sprite that was dwarfed by a Bentley on one side and an Escalade on the other.

"*This* is your car?"

"You don't like it?"

"It's just that it's so cute."

"Not something Clay Creighton would drive?"

Lara smiled and shrugged.

"The Fast Lane philosophy isn't just about power and speed," Clay gently explained. "It's also about what's unique and deserving."

"This car did set land speed records."

"Wow."

"What? A girl can't know something like that?"

"No, no—I approve. It's kind of sexy." Clay gazed into Lara's eyes as he opened the diminutive passenger-side door for her.

"That's good," Lara said as she settled into the seat, "because I also know this was the first Austin-Healey with a six-cylinder engine, and that it ran at Le Mans."

Clay stepped over the driver's side door to get in. "That's what makes this car cool." He tapped the ignition key to his temple. "It's tiny, but it *thinks* it's big."

* * *

Lara loved feeling the breeze in her hair as Clay drove them into Bel Air. She felt like a puppy with its head hanging out the window, its tongue lolling in the wind—except for the tongue part. She never got that feeling in her dowdy Taurus—even with all the windows rolled down. Having gusts smack your head from the sides was a poor imitation of the rush from a breeze slapping you square in the face over the top of a low-slung windshield like the Frogeye's.

Clay pulled the car into a Lexus dealership that looked more luxurious than a three-star Palm Springs hotel. Lara had never been in a three-star Palm Springs hotel, but she'd heard stories and seen pictures.

Oddly, not a single vehicle sat outside. "Where are all the cars?" Lara asked.

"Inside," Clay said. "Nothing's harder on a car's finish than the sun."

A man impeccably dressed in a Brioni suit exited the steel-gray building through a glass door made nearly opaque by UV-protective film.

"Mr. Creighton," the man said. "Your vehicle is waiting."

"This is the surprise?" Lara asked. "You're picking up a car?"

"Not just 'a' car, madam," the gentleman said. "Mr. Creighton is picking up his certified Lexus LFA."

Clay smiled. "Silvio, this is Lara."

"How do you do?" Silvio said, opting to bow instead of extending his hand. "As the owner of this establishment, I welcome you as a dear friend." He turned to Clay. "Are you ready?"

"Lead the way."

Silvio held the door for Lara and Clay. Lara had never heard of the car Clay was there to get, but it was easy to spot once they were inside. Parked on the slate of the showroom floor, the white two-seater gleamed as though bathed in the light of a hundred suns. Its triangular headlamps and air scoops behind each door made it look like a raptor.

"It looks like an eagle swooping down on its prey," Lara said.

"It is one sexy automobile," Clay said.

It is—if you think a bird swooping down on its prey is sexy.

"Your certificate, sir." Silvio presented an official-looking parchment to Clay.

"Certificate?" Lara wondered out loud.

"Yes, madam," Silvio said. "Lexus intends to limit ownership of the LFA to a very select few. One must be approved in advance—a mere formality in Mr. Creighton's case, of course."

"Of course."

An assistant, also impeccably dressed and wearing white gloves, approached carrying an inlaid wood box, which he opened and presented to Clay as though revealing the jewels of the crown. Instead, resting on red velvet, was a key fob.

Clay turned to Lara. "Ready for the ride of your life?"

* * *

Lara had seen plenty of fine performance vehicles when she attended races with her dad, but she had never been in a car like this LFA. Its powerful V-10 hummed as Clay zigzagged through traffic, heading east on the 10.

A Bugatti Veyron scorched past them as they were doing ninety just outside Calimesa. Lara looked at Clay to see how he'd react.

He laughed.

"That's a really nice car," he said.

"Nicer than this one?"

"This one's nice. But the Bugatti...that's a work of art."

"I don't know of any other 'work of art' that goes 200 miles an hour," Lara said.

"Now, you see—it's things like that."

"What?"

"Knowing how fast a car can go."

"I thought we settled this."

"Not because you're a woman. I'll bet ninety-nine percent of men wouldn't know a thing like that. Or how many cylinders a '57 Frogeye's engine had. Or what ran at Targa in 1960."

"A man who read your Driver blog might."

"How many men is that? One percent?"

Lara smiled and shrugged.

"So, you're a 'Driver'?" Clay continued.

"I keep up."

"Why?"

"Know your enemy and yourself."

Clay's eyes sparkled. "Ah, so you've bought into my theory?"

"It never hurts a woman to know what's going on in your beady little masculine brains."

"So, maybe I'm doing the human race more good than I realize."

"Don't get yourself a Tommy John injury patting yourself on the back. My dad used to take me with him to car races."

"Tommy John? You know baseball, too?"

"Geez—you think women don't follow sports? I played softball in high school, you know."

"Yeah, but Tommy John."

"I'm not talking about *the guy*. I'm talking about *the surgery*. Anyone can injure an elbow. Everyone's unemployed, we're fighting umpteen wars, the polar ice caps are melting, but you turn on the news in L.A. and the top story is about some celebrity gone wild, or a hundred-million-dollar pitcher who needs his elbow rearranged. Nothing's more important than how it's going with the Dodgers' rotation."

Rotation? Fuck! A wavelet of panic shot from Lara's chest to her head.

"Sports *is* big business," Clay said. "I mean, if you're paying a guy a hundred million dollars."

Whew.

Lara looked at the vibrant desert stretching out in all directions. Endless shades of red, brown and gray accented dusty green plants that thrived in spite of the environment.

"So," Clay said after a lull, "your father took you to car races?"

"Is that strange?"

"I don't know. Define 'strange.' My father was an international playboy."

Lara hated to abandon the caresses of the sun and the wind, but she turned to Clay.

"My dad...more or less...raised me on his own. After I turned seven."

"Oh."

"He took me to Pomona, Ontario, Bakersfield. He loved anything fast and loud. Stock cars. Formula One. Dragsters. We'd sit in the grandstand and he'd tell me all about whatever cars happened to be on the track. After a while, I picked up on things to where we could argue about which cars were faster, which handled better. I always cheered for the ones with the big horsepower."

"Yeah, that's important, but it all comes down to handling."

Lara's mouth dropped open. "That's what my dad always said."

"No kidding?"

"He said, 'What difference does it make if you're going two hundred m p h if you spin out in the curves?' That's how he said it: m...p...h."

Clay nodded.

"'There's no sense in stomping your foot to the floor,'" Lara said, "'if—'"

Clay took over. "'If you can't make the car go where you need it to go.'"

Lara looked surprised.

"My old man used to say that, too," Clay explained.

"Who would have thought our fathers..."

"My dad was a decent guy," Clay said, keeping his eyes on the road. "Most people don't know anything about him beyond his public persona. Their loss."

Lara studied Clay's face. She could almost read what he was thinking.

"I loved doing things with my dad," she said. "A little girl on an outing with her hero. He gave me everything I wanted: Popcorn. Hot dogs. Slushies. If I liked a hat, he'd buy it for me. He knew how to treat a lady."

Lara looked out the window. The colors that looked so amazingly distinct before now blew past in a blur.

"Your dad sounds like the kind of guy I'd like to meet," Clay said.

"Oh, um...he died."

"I'm sorry."

"No, it was a long time ago. When I was in high school."

"Yeah, but it's still a big thing. You two had something special."

"I didn't mean to turn this into a downer. I have lots of great memories. Probably more than most people. In his last few months, we'd just sit together and watch NASCAR. Sometimes not talking for hours."

They fell silent.

"You know, that's a great thing, just sitting and watching sports with someone," Clay finally said. "Most women don't understand how men can watch sports together without saying a thing, and then insist it was a great bonding experience."

"Anyway," Lara said, "you have a destination in mind, or are we just out cruising?"

"I thought we'd hit the salt flats near Whitewater, north of Bonnie Bell. We can put this baby through its paces there."

"Salt flats? Let's do it."

* * *

At Bonnie Bell, Clay exited the freeway and drove into a canyon that opened into the broad, flat bowl of a dried-up lake.

"I never knew about this place."

"Not a lot of people do."

There wasn't a soul in sight. Just white crust and gray-brown mountains.

Clay stopped the car. The engine purred. "Okay," he said, "here goes nuthin'."

Clay flicked the paddle shifter on the steering wheel and let the clutch snap. Lara felt like she'd been shot from a gun. The car was a sensual cornucopia. G-forces pressed her into the seat. The pistons wailed. She tasted salt on her tongue. The tachometer flickered as it tickled the red zone—nine-thousand rpm—each time Clay shifted.

As the car screamed past ninety mph, Lara closed her eyes and imagined they were on the verge of flying. And *then* Clay deposited the car into sixth and jammed the accelerator to the floor. Forces and decibels multiplied, and in a blink of an eye, they were doing one-ninety-three.

Lara checked the side-view mirror. It occurred to her that she should be frightened by the sight of dust billowing behind them. But as the ride pushed into atmospheres Lara had never experienced, she felt stimulated in new ways.

Clay slammed the brakes. The car decelerated rapidly but smoothly as he steered it into a perfect one-eighty, easing up on the brake a touch at the end to bring the car to a stop as soft and gentle as a silk baby blanket.

"Wow!" Lara exclaimed.

"Ready?"

"For what?"

"To take your turn."

Lara's jaw dropped. "I can't—"

But Clay had already turned off the engine, bounded from the vehicle and zipped around to open Lara's door.

"Can't what?" he said, reaching in to help her climb out.

"You had to apply just to get the car." Clay had already guided her halfway around to the driver's side.

"I gave them their money. I can do whatever I want with it."

"What if I...?" Lara dug in her heels as she peered into the supercar's cockpit.

"What?"

"Crash!"

"Look around." Clay spread his arms wide. "What're you going to hit? A mountain?"

Like that's not possible.

Lara eased into place behind the semicircular wheel. Leather trim made the curved top feel alive; the squared-off bottom looked like something out of *Star Wars*.

Clay jumped into the passenger seat and buckled his seat belt. "Okay. Let's see what she's got."

Me—or the car?

"But I've never driven anything like this before," Lara said.

"You went to all those races."

"And sat in the stands."

"Just have fun. It's the only reason a machine like this exists."

Easy for you to say.

Lara checked the mirrors and nervously opened and closed her fingers on the steering wheel.

"Really," Clay said, "it's not much different than whatever you normally drive."

Yes, it does have an engine and four wheels—just like my crappy Taurus.

"You haven't seen what I normally drive."

"It's got an engine and four wheels. Just give the engine some gas and point the wheels where you want them to go."

Another of her dad's isms.

"Um, these things..." Cringing at the thought of sounding like a dumb girl, Lara pointed to the paddle shifters on either side of the steering wheel.

"You can use the stick if you want."

"I'm a little out of practice."

"No problem." Clay pressed a button on the console and a knob rose into view, as if they were in a James Bond movie. Clay turned the knob until it pointed to the word "Auto."

"That should work."

Lara nodded as she depressed the starter switch. The car howled to life. Just tapping the gas pedal made it growl like an animal. An animal she controlled—she hoped. She gripped the wheel and stroked the leather. She took a deep breath and shifted the transmission to drive. A mere touch on the accelerator launched them like a rocket across the hard valley floor.

Lara remained cautious for the first few thousand feet. But even as it approached ninety, the car seemed to flow over the terrain. Smooth. Steady.

Okay so far.

"How's it feel?"

Great not to be in Junkerland for a change. "It almost drives itself."

"Give yourself more credit than that. You're going one-forty."

One-forty?

Lara wouldn't have believed it, but there it was on the digital display. She battled an impulse to yank her foot off the gas as she edged from exhilaration to ecstasy. She was Lara the Brave, living life, doing new things and liking it. She jammed the pedal almost to the floor, and the booster rockets kicked in. A new sensation, but she still felt in control.

Of the car. Of the situation. Of life in general.

The walls of the valley loomed closer with each passing second. Lara eased up on the gas and let the car cruise before applying the brake and bringing the car to a stop.

"All right!" Clay said. "You sure you never drove a vehicle like this before?"

"I never imagined."

"Want to try another setting?"

Lara looked at the selector knob, but she clutched the wheel too tightly to let go.

Clay grabbed the knob. "You've already done automatic. There's sport, normal and wet."

"What's the difference?"

"Pick one," Clay said. "We'll find out."

Clay's confidence gave Lara the confidence to focus more closely. "We're in the middle of the desert. What if..."

She twisted the knob to "wet" and gave Clay a matter-of-fact look.

"Why not?" Clay said. "This used to be a lake."

Lara looked over the tops of her sunglasses as she turned the knob to "sport." She palmed the floor shifter, licked her lips and pumped the gas pedal. The engine roared. The tachometer raged red. Lara let the clutch fly, initiating a new launch.

Dust filled the rear-view, only this time Lara had no doubts about how she should feel.

"So, how do you do a one-eighty?"

Clay provided a ten-second how-to. Lara dug her nails into the leather on the wheel as she mentally prepared for the maneuver. Then she stomped on the brake and forced the car into a skid. She almost overdid it, but her instinct to ease up just a tad corrected their course. The car spun around, ending up facing the way they had come.

Clay let out a whoop.

Lara's heart pounded as she ripped off her shades. "That was fucking awesome!" She put a hand over her mouth.

"I guess so, to warrant another F-bomb." Clay moved her hand away and kissed her.

* * *

Clay's lips were firm. He had not shaved, and Lara enjoyed the bristly feel on her cheeks. Clay tasted somewhat salty, too, a reminder of where they were at the moment.

But is it THE moment?

It seemed they were heading toward it. *This is a good thing. This is the plan.* Still, Lara found herself looking down when their

lips parted. Not to be demure. She was straining to stay cool. To avoid revealing what was going on in her head—and other parts of her body.

Clay broke the silence. "Well."

"Yes. Well."

Clay's hand dropped from Lara's face to her thigh, warming her leg as he stroked it through the thin cotton.

"This is getting to be a much more exciting day than I had originally planned," Clay said.

"What was your original plan?" Lara could feel his gaze, but still averted her eyes.

"Pick up a car. Drive around."

He kissed her neck. Right below the ear. *Ah, yes.* Lara closed her eyes and tilted her head back to make it easier for him. She felt herself sinking. Willingly. Into the car seat's embrace. Into a spell. Into the dark corners of her mind. Clay moved his hand along the curve of her hip to her waist.

Lara exhaled and sank even deeper. "What is your plan now?"

Clay tugged on the seat belt and grunted. "Tight fit in here," he said.

Watching as Clay's elbow bumped first the shifter, then the steering wheel, then the head rest, Lara could see things weren't likely to go much further in this setting.

Maybe the hood...

"I think we need a little space," she said.

Clay nodded and extricated himself from the cabin. Lara watched from her side of the car as he stretched out a charley horse in his shoulder.

"So, are you coming over here, or do I have to come over there?" he said with a sneaky smile.

"We could meet halfway," Lara responded, mimicking his look.

She nonchalantly moved forward to rest her arms on the foxy rake of the LFA's roof. But the blazing sun had cooked the steel there as hot as a stovetop, making Lara's next maneuver—a spastic recoil accompanied by a pitiful yelp—anything but nonchalant.

She rubbed her arms where they'd been scorched by the searing metal.

Clay zipped to her aid. "Are you okay?"

"Oh, geez, it's just a little—"

She couldn't even finish the sentence before Clay grunted.

"What's wrong?"

Clay rubbed a spot under his arm.

"Nothing..."

"No, what?"

He pushed gingerly between two ribs. "It's stupid. I wasn't paying attention and banged into the door."

"Does it hurt?"

"Forget it. Let me have a look here." Clay lifted Lara's arms so he could see the underside of her wrists. "Doesn't look so bad."

"Oh, now you're a doctor?"

"No. And I don't play one on TV," Clay said. "But this much I know: Scientific studies show that simply touching any part of a woman is good for a man's health. Elevates his heart rate."

"Fascinating. But who's the patient?"

"Good question." Clay kissed Lara on one wrist, then the other. Then he continued kissing her arm all the way to her shoulder.

Feeling better already...

Lara took a deep breath. Clay moved closer until his body pressed against hers. And then pressed her body against the gutter that ran along the roofline above the car door, giving Lara a clear notion of what it must feel like to be branded. She jerked forward, ramming Clay's nose with her shoulder.

"Omigod! I'm so sorry!"

Clay's lips moved, but his face was clenched so tightly that no words came out.

"Are you bleeding?"

"No—no. Just a little bump." Clay opened his eyes as far as he could in an attempt to illustrate his point. "See? Good as—"

He sneezed.

Lara yelped again.

"That was suave." Clay daubed Lara's cheek with his sleeve. "I'll have to add that to the Pit Stop Blog: 'How not to blow it by sneezing on your date.'"

Lara burst out laughing. "It is a fun car, but it's got its drawbacks."

"I'll use that line in my review."

Lara stopped laughing when she saw a dime-size spot of blood on Clay's shirt. "You *are* hurt."

The sight of the crimson circle only made Clay laugh harder. "I've been going through a lot of shirts since I met you."

Lara gave him a playful push. "So I guess it doesn't hurt?"

"Pain's all in the head," Clay said. "And right now, I'm focused on other things."

He put his hands on Lara's hips and drew her to him. She put her hands on his shoulders and turned her head to accommodate his kiss. But just as she closed her eyes, her upper arm grazed that damned branding iron of a gutter.

"Fuck!"

Clay looked stunned. Lara turned red.

"Oh, my," she said. "Another F-bomb. Not particularly ladylike."

"What *is* the ladylike reaction to being burned by a car roof?" Clay checked out Lara's elbow. "Looks red. Maybe we—"

"Should go somewhere else?" *Oh, my god—too far! I mean, how obvious?*

"Good idea," Clay said. "I know a place."

SIX

*C*lay drove back to the 10, but instead of heading toward L.A., he took the eastbound ramp toward Palm Springs.

A good sign.

Palm Springs was home to Clay's infamous Heat resort. The suites had names like Coyote, Arroyo, Chollo and Casino, where, according to legend, Fast Lane guaranteed well-heeled male guests they would get lucky.

"Shouldn't we be going the other way?" she said.

"Depends on where you're trying to end up."

The Casino Room? Lara didn't say anything. She didn't want to jinx anything by talking too much.

And then there was the scenery. The sun dipped behind the mountains, turning them purple. Even in the ebbing luster of daytime, the desert was a feast of colors and textures. Lights sparkled in the distance,

and then silhouettes of palm trees and stately buildings appeared, etched into the deepening blue of the
cloudless sky.

"Beautiful, isn't it?" Clay asked. "People think it'll
be like Vegas...lights flashing everywhere. Not that
that's a bad thing, if you're in the mood."

The Heat sign came into view.

"So, where are we going?" Lara said, playing
innocent.

"Right over there." Clay pulled into the circle drive
in front of the resort.

"A hotel? Come here often?"

"Yes, actually. I own it."

"How handy."

Clay stopped in front of the ornate art deco entry-
way, sprang from the vehicle, danced over to Lara's
side and nabbed the door handle just as the deeply
tanned valet got there.

"Mr. C?"

"Ricky! How's business this evening?"

"You know. The usual." Ricky looked nervously
over his shoulder toward the lobby. He turned pale
when Clay opened the car door for Lara.

Clay nodded toward the hotel. "I'm betting everyone's going to be surprised to see me."

"Yes, sir. I think you would win that bet."

Clay discreetly produced a hundred-dollar bill and
handed it to Ricky. "Have fun parking this baby."

"I think I will, sir. Quite a beauty."

"Yes, she is," Clay said. "And the car's pretty hot, too."

Smiling devilishly at Lara, he crooked his arm. She clasped it, and together they headed inside.

* * *

The lobby was bigger than entire hotels Lara had stayed in. Palatial, yet understated. Earth tones every-where. And glass—lots of it, creating the illusion that the inside of the building and the landscape flowed seamlessly together.

Lara became aware of a growing hubbub. A young woman and an older man in identical suits hustled toward them.

"Donald, Therese, how are you this evening?"

"Very well, Mr. C," Therese responded. "We weren't expecting you."

"But now that I'm here, I'm sure Sushma—" He was interrupted by the squawk of Therese's phone.

"Yes, Ms. V, a few minutes ago." She held the phone out to Clay. "Ms. V would like to speak with you, sir."

Clay took the phone and turned on the speaker. "Hey. Nice evening."

"Nice evening, my Brahmin ass. Now, turn off that speaker."

"But, Shush, I—"

"Do not 'Shush' me. Turn off the speaker."

"But, it would be rude—"

"I will be more than happy to provide you lessons in the true meaning of the word 'rude.'"

Clay looked at Lara and shrugged. "Do you mind? My associate seems to be having issues."

"You will be having my knee to your balls if you do not turn off that speaker pronto!"

Lara threw up her hands in mock resignation. "You'd better do what she says."

"Be right with you, Ms. V." Clay turned off the speaker. "Donald and Therese, this is Lara Dixon. D and T are two of my best. They'll set you up while I take care of this. Is The Coyote available?"

"I'm afraid not, sir," Donald answered, "but the Oasis..."

Therese looked as though she might puke.

"Even better," Clay said. He winked at Lara and turned away.

Therese elbowed Donald in the ribs. "Nice work, moron," she whispered a little too loudly. "Maybe Ms. V should apply her knee to *your* balls."

Lara turned around, pretending not to have heard. "So...the Oasis?"

"Yes, Miss Dixon," Therese said, suddenly congenial. "This is your first time here, yes?"

Lara knew that they would know if she had been

to Heat before. Under her own name, at least. The resort was renowned as a haven where no questions were asked of familiar faces checking in under not-so-familiar names, but Lara did not have a familiar face.

"Yes, actually, it is."

"Excellent. I'm sure you'll enjoy the accommodations."

"No doubt."

"Please."

Donald and Therese herded Lara toward the gilded front desk—and then whisked past it and into a private elevator.

* * *

The Oasis Suite was the only room more notorious than the Casino Suite. Reserved for elite guests. Movie stars. Politicians. Super Bowl MVPs. And whoever accompanied them.

The décor had a Middle Eastern feel. In the bedroom, one wall was made entirely of glass with no apparent curtains or blinds. An exhibitionist's paradise? Lara couldn't see any lights shining in the darkness outside. No buildings. No streetlights. No lines of cars. She cupped her hands, pressed them against the window and looked through them like binoculars, but she could barely discern the stark outlines of mountains.

And then she turned and contemplated the waterfall.

At twelve feet tall, it towered above the golden spider marble floor. It would have been imposing, but water splashed soothingly from a highly believable-looking outcropping of rock onto a ledge before spilling into a pool as big as a party-size Jacuzzi. Exotic plants thrived in crevices and ledges.

Therese clicked off her phone as she came into the bedroom from the living room. "Do you like it?"

"I don't know how to describe—"

"It has that effect on people. Now, about your luggage…"

"I don't actually have any."

"I see," Therese said, not missing a beat. "You'll need toiletries and such. I'll have a basket sent up. Do you have any preferences? Soap? Shampoo? A certain line of makeup?"

"No, I'm easy." *Nice word choice.*

Therese didn't bat an eyelash. "Our fashion concierge can get you outfitted for dinner."

"You have a 'fashion concierge'?"

"Of course."

Just like that. "I don't think that'll be necessary."

"I understand you've been to the salt flats today."

"How did you know that?"

Therese ran a finger over one of the straps on Lara's dress. It came up coated in white powder.

"Oh."

"Actually, I was tipped off," Therese said. "It's a close-knit corporation, and every employee is issued a phone. Word gets around fast."

Oh, my god, I'm swimming in a fishbowl. "Huh," Lara said. "About the waterfall..."

"It's a fully functioning shower and hot tub." Therese went up to the base. "The temperature controls are hidden behind the ginger plant."

Lara's eyes scanned the waterfall. *Convenient.*

"It's the one with the pink stems and green-and-white striped leaves," Therese said. "The leaves look like feathers, but it's a tough plant. Just reach in."

Lara nodded.

"There's a nice selection of sleepwear in the closet." Therese threw open the closet door to reveal a treasure trove of negligees, none of which looked conducive to sleep. "If you don't like anything here, the concierge can help you with that, too."

"Great."

"Any questions?"

Lara shook her head.

"Okay, then. Chartre will give you a call." Therese pronounced it Shar-tray.

"Chartre?"

"The fashion concierge. Good night, Miss Dixon."

Therese turned to go. Lara looked at the glass wall. "Actually, I do have one more question."

Therese followed the line of Lara's gaze. "I know. It seems like you're in a fishbowl. Believe me, you can see out, but no one can see in. There's not much of a view right now, but if you get real close, you can just barely see the outline of the mountains." She did what Lara had done earlier, cupping her hands like binoculars on the glass. Lara did it, too.

"So, no worries about taking a shower?" Lara sounded unsure.

"No worries about taking a shower. And if you've been to the salt flats, a shower's a good idea." Therese smiled and left.

Lara studied the waterfall. *A shower* is *a good idea.*

* * *

Lara peeled the yellow dress from her body, raising a cloud of white powder. Her skin had been scoured where salty grit had become trapped in her bra and underwear. She started peeling those off, too, but the gaping blackness of the massive window gave her pause. She walked up to the window and gave it a tap. *Therese said no one could look in. Why would she say it if it wasn't true?* Lara's eyes traced the edges of the glass. *And what if it wasn't true?*

Lara reached behind her and unclasped her bra. Be bold. Lara slid the straps down over her arms and let

the bra fall to the floor. She took a deep breath. *Okay.*
She tucked her thumbs into the elastic and pulled her
lacy hip huggers to her ankles. And then stepped out
of them. Right there in front of the window.

*If anyone's looking, I hope they're not
disappointed.*

Lara's phone rang. It was Clay.

"Hey," she said.

"What's up?"

"Oh...nothing." *Literally.*

"Like the room?"

"It's really something."

"You know the waterfall's a natural outcropping of
rock."

"Really?" Lara stroked the rock. It looked smooth,
but felt grainy.

"The very first time I visited the site I knew it had
to be incorporated into a room somehow."

"But, the water..."

"That's man-made."

"The *water* is man-made?"

"There's a pump."

"I see." Lara moved close enough to touch the
water. It was warm and smacked the back of her hand
like rain.

"Any plans for tonight?"

Maybe. "I apparently have an appointment with
your fashion concierge."

"Ah, Chartre. You'll like him."

"Him?"

"Therese didn't tell you?"

"It's hard to tell from the name." Lara noticed a cache of downy towels tucked behind the ginger plant.

"How about dinner? In, say, fifteen minutes?"

"What about Chartre?"

"You can meet with Chartre some other time."

"I don't know if what I have on is acceptable for dinner here."

"Don't worry. It's a casual place."

Lara discovered that two of what she thought were towels were actually big fluffy robes. "Okay."

"See you in fifteen."

She held a robe up in front of her and checked out her reflection in the wall of glass. "I'll be here."

* * *

The doorbell rang twelve minutes later. Lara answered it wearing nothing but one of the big fluffy robes.

Clay raised an eyebrow. "Am I early?"

"Actually, you're right on time." Lara pulled him into the room, pressed him against the closed door and kissed him deeply. He wore a clean, crisp shirt. His face was freshly shaven. He smelled like he had just stepped out of the shower.

"Why would you think you're early?"

"It's just—is that what you're wearing to dinner?"

"More or less. You?"

Lara untucked Clay's shirt and undid the buttons. Clay smelled her hair and planted baby kisses in the line where it parted.

The shirt hung open, revealing Clay's toned torso. In his blogs, Clay had encouraged men to emulate the build of a wide receiver. Lara didn't think she could tell the difference between a wide receiver and a second baseman, but she certainly liked what she was seeing. And touching. She undid the belt on the robe, pressed her bare chest into Clay's, and kissed him again.

"What about dinner?"

"I haven't showered yet," Lara said as she headed toward the bedroom. "And we did spend that time at the salt flats."

She let the robe drop just as she slipped through the door.

* * *

Lara dimmed the main lights and stepped onto the naked rock beneath the waterfall. In the subtle glow of strategically placed multicolored LEDs, with water splashing all around her, she felt as if she was on display for Clay's pleasure. An audience of one: It felt right.

She reached for a bottle of shampoo, but her hand met Clay's.

"That is a fine product," he said, "but I think this one will give your hair a more lustrous shine." He held up a clear bottle filled with a golden liquid that matched the amber sparkle in his eyes.

The touch of his bare legs on hers. His hand pressing lightly on the small of her back. The spotlights turning rivulets of water into a deluge of glittering diamonds. Yes, this was the right time. The right place.

"So, you're a media mogul, a doctor *and* a hairdresser?"

"I'm not licensed as one, nor do I play one on TV." Clay dispensed a generous dollop of shampoo into his palm. "But I have a feel for this kind of thing."

He laced the rich lather into Lara's hair, starting at her brow and combing his fingers through her drenched locks all the way to where they ended between her shoulder blades. As he softly massaged her scalp, foam drizzled down Lara's neck, shoulders and arms. When a few errant bubbles drifted toward her eyes, Clay deftly deflected them.

"Disaster averted," he said.

Lara turned to face him. "Good idea, putting a waterfall in this room."

They kissed as water danced all over their bodies. Froth cascaded down Lara's back, providing a sensuous contrast to the relative roughness of Clay's circling hands.

He pushed Lara against the rock and kissed her neck, then her shoulders, then her breasts, circling the edge of one nipple, then the other with his tongue. Lara shifted a little in hopes of making it clear that more direct contact would be perfectly acceptable.

To her delight, he interpreted the cue correctly.

Lara stroked Clay's hair as he made sure he gave each breast equal time. His hands traced the outlines of her body, coasting from her ribs to her hips and back up again, until he grabbed her ass firmly to lift her onto a ledge that quite conveniently stuck out from the other layers of limestone.

And then he dropped to his knees.

Clay stroked Lara's thighs as he tenderly licked between her legs. The Fast Lane Rule of the Road No. 1 was to make a woman feel like she's the center of the universe, and, little by little, Clay got closer and closer to the center of Lara's. His intensity increased along with her pulse rate and breathing. Lara absentmindedly let her hands roam over her own body

Clay lifted Lara's leg and then caressed it with his tongue down her thigh, past her knee, all the way to the middle of her calf. It tickled a little, even with the water flowing over them. Clay's eyes shone through drops of water like golden light through the prisms of a crystal chandelier. He propped the leg up on his shoulder, then retraced the path his tongue had taken.

"Don't let anything I'm doing down here stop you from whatever you're doing up there," he said.

Losing herself in the moment, Lara continued caressing herself—as much for her own benefit as for Clay's. Her elevator fantasy—with streams of water buffeting them—was coming to life. No mirrors on the ceiling—but Lara saw their reflection in the glass wall, bathed in dark light, engulfed in smoky shadows.

Clay stood up, pressed against Lara and kissed her hard. Their tongues danced around each other's, and as they separated, Lara caught Clay's lower lip between her teeth, releasing it with a flick of her tongue.

They looked into each other's eyes. Clay moved his hips so that he teasingly nudged hers as he reached to a point just behind Lara's ear. Curious, Lara looked over her shoulder and saw Clay reach into another cranny and pull out—a condom!

Lara's mouth fell open.

"Comes with the room," Clay said matter-of-factly. "Compliments of the host."

He ripped open the packaging with his teeth, extricated the rubber and slipped it into place in one smooth motion.

Very smooth. How many times has he done that?

Lara didn't have much time to ponder the question as Clay eased her back onto the ledge. Then he eased himself into her with slow, deliberate strokes. Not that Lara needed him to go slow, but she appreciated his thoughtfulness.

Lara could feel the blood coursing through his member. Or was that her own pulse? She couldn't tell as they moved and breathed in unison. Everything sped up. Clay slid his hands beneath Lara, cupping her buttocks to pull her up and toward him with each thrust. Lara stretched out her arms to anchor herself. The blood rushing in her ears drowned out the roar of the shower. Her breathing got shallower until she could barely inhale. And barely needed to.

Clay pushed into her as far as he could go. They were moving at a hundred miles per hour—and then everything suddenly stopped. For a moment, everything hung in suspended animation. Lara's whole body tensed. Her fingers dug into clefts in the rock.

And then torrents of pleasure cascaded to every part of her body.

They let go simultaneously, shuddered, then leaned against each other, panting, languid. The sound of the waterfall returned.

Lara's eyes fluttered open to meet Clay's gilded gaze. *A shower* was *a pretty good idea.*

SEVEN

*A*n hour later Lara lay on her side on the vast bed, her naked skin drinking in the milky smoothness of the silk sheets, Clay drawing circles on her shoulders with his fingers. A girl could get used to this.

"More Veuve Clicquot?"

Lara turned toward Clay. *A girl could get used to this, too.* She kissed him. He tasted like pineapple and champagne.

"It might be easier if I pour it into a flute."

"But not as much fun." *Be careful. Don't have too much fun.*

Clay turned to the remains of a midnight snack tray of fruit, cheese and exotic crackers and refilled two flutes with bubbly. Lara took a sip and let it linger on her tongue while she pondered the bottle's unassuming—almost generic—yellow label. Clay had assured her the Veuve Clicquot balanced power and delicacy better than vintages that cost three times as much.

Sure beats Andre.

"A penny for your thoughts," Clay said.

"Just one penny?"

"A million?"

"That's still only ten thousand dollars. How much did you pay for the car you bought today?"

"I withdraw all offers. Your thoughts are priceless, anyways."

Some of them, maybe. "Okay. I was wondering why there's a nice selection of lingerie in that closet."

"Some of my guests can be impulsive."

"The host, too?"

"Me? No. I never stay in this room."

"You don't?"

"It's reserved for good friends."

"Tonight?"

"I don't know. I haven't been invited."

Lara looked off to the side and sipped her champagne.

"Like it?" Clay emptied the bottle by topping off both of their glasses.

"I haven't decided yet." She took another sip. "What was the other choice?"

"La Grand Dame Riva. I could have some sent up." He reached for his phone.

"Don't do that. There's no way we could finish it."

"Who says we have to finish it?"

"You said it cost five hundred dollars a bottle."

114

"I have a whole case."

"Maybe another time."

Clay shrugged and put down the phone.

"All this is kind of outrageous," Lara said. "Expensive wine. Indoor waterfalls in the middle of the desert. A closet full of nighties."

"I outdid myself on this room," Clay said without a hint of smugness.

"Everything's pretty enough."

"Something tells me there's a 'but' coming."

"But it's kind of self-indulgent."

"That's the whole point of a place like this."

"It seems so wasteful."

"Emphasis on *seems*."

Lara gave him a prove-it look.

"All the stone," he said, "every bit of it, came from right here, onsite. All the wood is repurposed—some of it's from old-growth forests that were harvested in the 1880s. The way the building's set into the hillside—and the fact that every inch of glass is insulated and polarized—means there's no air-conditioning."

"But, the fountains and the waterfall..."

"The water's recycled. Even the stuff that evaporates." He pointed to unassuming fixtures tucked away in the shadows of the rafters. "Humidity collectors. We've lost only one percent of the original water since we opened five years ago."

"All the self-indulgence, none of the guilt."

"I like that. Maybe I should hook you up with our ad people."

"So, my thoughts turned out to be worth a penny after all?"

"Absolutely. And I would shell out a lot more to get inside your head and take a good look around."

"What do you think you'd find?"

"Mysteries."

"Like what? Secrets of my dark, sordid past?"

"Oh, no. My security people will take care of that." His matter-of-fact tone gave Lara pause. "I'm talking about being able to see what makes you think the things you think and do the things you do."

"If you could just somehow get inside there and roam around a little, you'd be able to figure that all out?"

"Probably not."

"Then what would be the point?"

"You're right. It's better not to know everything about someone. If you did, you might not want to know them anymore."

Oh, shit. Just stay cool. Lara turned back onto her side so Clay couldn't see her face. "You, um, you hear about people having 'a meeting of the minds.'"

"Yeah, but how much do you really know? I mean, take Sushma and me. We've got a meeting of the minds about how to run Fast Lane. But it's all about business. We come to work, do our jobs, go home at night."

Clay had made circles on Lara's shoulder again, but now he rolled onto his back.

"My dad had a passion for this business. He tried to instill that in me—really wanted me to have what he had. I guess it just wasn't in my genes. He drove this place with his heart. I was in over my head."

Lara rolled over to look at Clay. He looked at the ceiling.

"By the time Shush came along, Fast Lane had missed the curve and was heading for the wall. She proposed all kinds of things I never heard of—I still don't know what they all were. But I had a feeling she could turn things around. And she did. But for all the work we've done together, I really don't know much about her."

He looked at Lara. "All business."

Lara made circles on his shoulder. "That conversation I heard in the lobby was 'all business'?"

"She's gotten this reputation as the mother hen of Fast Lane. But she's more like a surrogate dad. To me, at least. A cool dad you can joke around with."

I tried to get that out of a husband. Big mistake. "I never heard anyone talking with their father the way you talk to Shushma."

"Soosh-ma." Clay chuckled. "I call her Shush because she can be, well, a little excitable. I'm the only person in the world who can get away with that."

"She did sound pretty angry."

117

"It drives her crazy when I go off the radar like I did today."

"Couldn't she just call you on your company-issue phone?"

"I turned it off."

"Why?"

"I didn't want to be interrupted—I didn't want us to be interrupted."

Clay turned toward Lara. Her heart beat faster. *Those eyes.*

"She's kind of afraid of you, you know," Clay continued.

"Of *me*?" Lara felt a flash of panic. She sat up and turned away. "Why would she be afraid of *me*?"

"You came out of nowhere. She doesn't know anything about you, and that scares her. Knowledge is power, and if she doesn't know anything about you, she feels like she's not in control."

"What does she think there is to know?"

"It's S.O.P, that's all. I'm a brand. What I do affects people's lives. At least, that's what Shush tells me. Over and over. I'm not so good at, you know, the details, so I employ other people who are. Everything—and everyone—has to check out." He sat up and put a hand on her shoulder. "You're not intimidated by that?"

"Oh, no!" Lara looked at him over her shoulder. "A little, I guess."

"I forget. I grew up in a fishbowl, so I hardly notice it."

Fishbowl. How easy would it be for someone to link me to Gina? "What is she trying to find out about me?"

"The usual stuff. If you have a criminal record. A history with any terrorist organizations or cults. Ties to some competitor, maybe a tell-all media organization. You can't be too careful about corporate sabotage. Some companies will do just about anything."

"You don't sound too worried."

"It's not my job to be worried."

"What *is* your job?"

"My job is to be Clay Creighton." He kissed his way from one of Lara's shoulders to the other.

Oh, my god...is he on the clock right now?

Clay stopped abruptly. "Oh! You have marks from the car!"

"I have what?"

"Do they hurt?"

"Do *what* hurt?"

"I know just the thing." Clay sprang from the bed and bounded to the basket of lotions and creams next to the hot tub. Lara craned her neck but couldn't see any marks, so she felt around with her fingers.

"Uh...uh. Don't irritate it." Clay sat close to Lara

and rubbed a velvety salve onto her back. "Feels good, right?" he said. "Soothing."

Since Lara hadn't even known about the marks, there wasn't really anything to soothe. But she didn't mind Clay doing what he was doing.

EIGHT

The second lovemaking session with Clay had begun with him, as he had said, being himself. Which meant, as far as Lara could tell, "irresistible," "charming," "attentive" and more of a man than she had ever experienced. It began with the cream and the kisses and ended up with her on her back with Clay more or less nailing her to the mattress. She hadn't experienced that since the second year of her seven-year marriage. Maybe even the first.

Like falling off a bike—except that if falling off a bike felt so good, people would do it on purpose. Afterward, though thoroughly spent after the day in the sun and the evening with Clay, Lara found it difficult to sleep. Lying in the dark with Clay pressing against her, his breathing rhythmic and deep, and hearing nothing but the waterfall's murmur, Lara mulled over the many ways in which Clay had sur prised her. Is there a soul somewhere beneath those ripped abs and that infectious smile?

Still, casting a pall over everything was this business of The Rotation. If Clay did, indeed, have a soul, what darkness in his character allowed him to indulge himself in such a travesty?

Black and white tigers. A supercar that could go two hundred miles per hour. Sex in a waterfall. A glass bedroom. The waterfall. Expensive champagne.

The waterfall.

Eventually, the waterfall and exhaustion won out. The next thing Lara heard was a phone ringing.

* * *

It was Clay's. Still not fully awake, Lara looked at him and blinked. Clay mouthed one word: "Chartre."

"Ask when's a good time."

"When's a good time? He says now."

"*Now*?" Lara sat up and held the sheet in front of her chest.

"I don't think she's on the same page. What's this all about, calling at this ungodly time of day? Oh. He says you had an appointment."

Now Lara was fully awake. "I thought the appointment was for ten."

"He says it is ten."

There was a knock on the door to the suite.

"And now someone's at the door?"

"That would be Chartre."

"What?"

"Right outside the door."

"Tell him to come back!"

Clay winced. "Ooh. You do not want to break a date with Chartre."

The knocking grew more insistent. Lara jumped out of bed, yanking the sheet along with her. "But I have to..." She fussed with her hair in the reflection of the glass wall.

"You have to what?"

"Get dressed." She checked her breath. "Brush my teeth."

"But he's here to dress you."

Lara realized she could see through the glass wall. A pool. A golf course. Desert. There were no people in view, but Lara hiked the sheet all the way to her shoulders.

Clay pushed the sheet back down and kissed her shoulder. "Relax. Even if there was anyone out there, they couldn't see you." He wrapped a towel around his waist. "And there's nothing you could do to make yourself any more desirable, either."

The knocking got even more emphatic. Clay kissed Lara's neck and then headed into the outer rooms. "Chill out! Geez!"

Lara looked at her reflection and saw herself wearing a sheet and suffering from a serious case of bed-head. *I look like the Statue of Liberty after a one-night stand.*

* * *

Out in the suite, Clay threw open the door to a pudgy little bald man wearing purple sweats, silver cross-trainers and Buddy Holly glasses with diamond-studded temples.

"Ten A of M, people!" Chartre trundled past Clay. Two female assistants—a blonde with long, straight hair and a redhead with her curls in a ponytail—followed, doing their best to avert their eyes as they passed their scantily clad boss.

"But we haven't even had breakfast," Clay said.

"Make that ten oh-one," Chartre countered. "And I can't imagine what you could have been doing to delay breakfast for so long." Chartre looked Clay up and down over the tops of his glasses as though noticing for the first time that he wore nothing more than a strategically placed band of terrycloth. "Then again, I have a pretty good guess. But what is that to me? I've been working since seven. The luxuries of a leisurely lifestyle do not trickle down to my level on the organizational chart."

"It's easy being C.E.O., huh? People barging in

on you on Sunday morning and making outrageous demands at such ungodly hours?"

"I'm not making any demands on *you*. I'm here to see Miss Dixon." He strode toward the bedroom.

"I'm not sure she's ready," Clay said as the assistants edged past him.

"Ten-oh-two!" Chartre disappeared through the door.

* * *

Lara preened in the smoked glass of the wall. She wore a negligee from the closet that resembled the swan gown Bjork wore to the Oscars. And it was at least six sizes too big. Lara pinched the plunging bodice to keep from flopping out.

"Good morning." Lara played it cool.

Chartre froze and stared at her. His face was stern, his lips taut, his eyes oddly impassive as they bored through her. Flanking Chartre, the assistants whipped out their phones so they would be ready to take notes when the Great Man spoke.

"The raw materials are all present," he said.

Lara frowned. "What does that mean?"

"He's saying you make a nice clothes rack," Clay explained as he sauntered in. Lara felt her face redden. Clay stood behind her with his hands on her shoulders. "He wants you to believe he has everything under control."

"Don't listen to him!" Chartre retorted. "I know what a woman's got. Although, I can't for the life of me fathom why, of all the wonderful negligees in that closet, anyone your size would choose this monstrosity."

It was the closest to my hand when I reached into the closet.

"Eight," Chartre barked to the assistants without looking at either of them. The redhead nodded and typed on her phone.

Chartre turned toward Clay. "Scoot!" he said, fanning Clay away with the back of his hand. Then he circled Lara, studying her as if she were a dog in a kennel show. She had the distinct impression he was judging her haunches, muzzle and coat—not good, since at the moment she felt more like a beagle than a greyhound. It was a strange position to be in, but it got stranger when, without warning, Chartre reached into the swan costume, hefted one of Lara's breasts with the back of a hand, then tweaked it to see how it bounced.

Lara squeaked, jumped back and raised her hand to slap Chartre, but Clay stopped her.

"It's okay. He's a professional," Clay whispered through gritted teeth.

Without acknowledging Lara's discomfort or Clay's admonition, Chartre tilted his head, puckered his lips and nodded.

"Yes, very nice raw materials," he said. "It will be wonderful dressing a woman. A *real* woman, if you know what I mean."

Not really.

Clay cupped his hands on his chest and whispered, "Natural."

In that case, all right.

Chartre nodded with scorn at the yellow dress that had made Lara feel so pretty the previous afternoon. The blond worker bee whisked it away as though removing roadkill from a highway.

"Are you going to get on with it," Clay chided, "or is she going to have to go around naked all day?

"We certainly wouldn't want *that*." Chartre clapped, and more assistants wheeled several racks of clothes into the room.

Lara was dumbfounded. "Do we really need all this?"

"My dear," Chartre said, looking at Lara over the top of his glasses, "we do things right around here."

* * *

Lara tried on one item after another. Chartre operated like a madman, tossing articles of clothing hither and yon, so focused that he practically ripped articles he deemed unacceptable from Lara's body before she had a chance to remove them. It made Lara giddy. So giddy that she blocked out Chartre and the worker bees. She was putting on a show for Clay—and he was enjoying it.

"Gina?"

Gina?

"Gina, love, where did this end up?" Chartre held up a pouffy turquoise chiffon top that no one but a seventeen-year-old suburbanite would wear.

The blond assistant feathered her phone's screen with her thumb. "Consider," she said.

"Consider? Whatever could I have been thinking?"

Gina. If Lara developed genuine feelings for Clay, how would that affect her "mission"? *And what's going on with him?* As she looked back over the past twenty-four hours, Lara could see how she might reinterpret certain utterances, certain moves, certain touches. Could it be possible that Clay—Clay Creighton, the ruler of the Fast Lane empire of plea-sure for men—might be feeling like a boy in a tux and a boutonniere slow-dancing with his favorite girl at the junior prom?

"I mean, really." Chartre tossed the offending gar-ment aside like a used dish rag. "I damn well better be at the top of my game if we're going to give this lovely creature a fitting welcome into The Rotation."

What?

Lara looked at Clay. "What?"

"That's a good question."

"Oh, dear." For the first time since Lara met him, Chartre was at a loss for words.

Clay, who had been reclining on the bed, stood up. "Are you saying Shush went ahead and..."

The color drained from Chartre's face. "All I know is that I was told this was a Rotation fitting."

A brusque voice came from near the door. "You were told correctly."

Everyone turned to see Sushma standing in the doorway, her arms crossed. "And, you are correct that everyone"—she shot a venomous glance at Clay—"had better be at the top of his game."

Sushma crossed the room toward Lara. Looking at Lara but talking to Clay, she said, "My, but she is as lovely as I have been led to believe. I am Sushma Vishnuveda."

She extended her hand.

NINE

*Y*ou do brighten a room, Shush," Clay said.

Sushma ignored Clay. "How is the fitting going, Miss Dixon?"

Fitting?

"You know, it might have been a good idea to ask Lara about it first."

"Why? Is this not what she wanted? Miss Dixon, is this not what you wanted?"

"I hadn't really thought about being in The Rotation." Lara felt her training on how to lie kicking into high gear.

"Apparently, doing things without thinking is quite in fashion around here." Sushma directed her deadpan gaze at Clay. "We need to talk."

"My schedule's pretty open all afternoon," Clay responded.

"Your schedule is open right now." Sushma marched toward the door.

"I'm not exactly dressed."

Sushma stopped. "I have seen you wearing less." She looked coyly in Lara's direction. Taking it as a show of dominance, Lara countered by tilting her head, narrowing her eyes and staring back at Sushma.

You may have been here first but I'm here now.

"Now's as good a time for a business meeting as any, I guess." Clay shrugged and gave Lara a peck on the cheek.

Chartre exhaled after Sushma and Clay were gone. "That was awkward," he said. "Where were we?" The blond assistant named Gina brought him a knee-length dress.

"Don't worry, my dear." Chartre held the dress up to Lara. "I'm sure you're going to love being a part of The Rotation. All the girls do."

He shook his head and tossed the dress aside.

* * *

Sushma followed Clay into the living room and shut the door behind her.

"Whatever happened to work/life balance?" Clay quipped.

"Do you think the paparazzi have heard of work/life balance?"

She pressed a button on her phone and handed it

to Clay. He watched a video of his and Lara's bungling attempts to hook up on the salt flat.

"Not exactly triple-X material," he said.

"No, but it is material that we cannot control—and your ill-considered escapade at Rev already has people asking whether this woman is Sun's replacement."

"I guess we know the answer to that question. So she checks out?"

"I have not been able to have her fully vetted."

Clay chewed on his lower lip. "Okay, you got me. No one gets into The Rotation without being fully vetted, but you just stuck Lara into The Rotation *because* she's not fully vetted?"

"You and your public antics with her gave me no choice."

"Now I get it. It's easier to keep an eye on her if she's on the inside."

Sushma just looked at him with gunslinger eyes.

Clay tightened the towel around his waist. "What if she doesn't check out? What if she was arrested for prostitution when she was fifteen, like Miriamne?"

"You do not know what goes on right before your very eyes!" Sushma waved her hands in Clay's face. "The arrest was not the only issue with Miriamne. It was the fact that she turned out to be only seventeen. And even though we found out before she was officially announced, it took a supreme effort to prevent her from becoming a serious problem."

Clay studied Sushma's face. *There's something fishy about this.* "I know what's really going on," he said. "You're scared."

"Scared of what?" Anger flashed in Sushma's eyes.

"You're worried things are going to change around here."

"Change I can contend with." She jabbed Clay's chest. "But she is a cipher, and that is a very bad sign. It is as if she has taken pains to cover her tracks."

Clay rubbed the red mark Sushma's fingernail made on his chest. "She was married to a movie producer! You know all about that."

"A B-movie producer, which is another thing I do not like about her. Her husband made tawdry films, and she was surprised to discover him cavorting with bimbos in a hot tub?"

"She's, I don't know...sweet."

"'Sweet'? Oh, my fucking god, can you even hear yourself speaking?"

"What's wrong with sweet?"

"'Sweet' is just one more reason to be suspicious. I have never met anyone 'sweet' whom I could trust."

Clay laughed and plopped into a big, soft chair.

"So you think—what? That Lara's some devious she-devil who's putting on an act to lull me into complacency? A Trojan horse bent on destroying me? Why?"

"I can think of one-point-two billion reasons."

"You are a piece of work, Shush. So hard-boiled and cynical."

"Cynical, worldly wise—call it what you will, Clayton Albert Creighton. My eyes are open."

"Everyone around me is so 'worldly wise.' That's what's so fascinating about Lara. She's naïve."

"A resounding endorsement."

"It's not an endorsement. It's refreshing." *Beat that.*

Sushma calmly checked her phone. "A pool of water can appear to be refreshing on a hot day," she said without looking at Clay, "but that does not make it a good idea to dive in head-first without knowing its depth."

Damn!

Clay looked at the floor. He knew that, from a business standpoint, Sushma was right. He had started to think Lara could be the woman who would end The Rotation. But, in business, one must proceed with caution. If bringing Lara to Rev and being seen with her at the salt flats had triggered an avalanche of speculation, it would be better for Fast Lane to make Lara official, hope for the

best, and dispatch her if a problem arose. That way, it would look as though Lara had deceived them, and that would corral valuable sympathy points from the media. Cold-hearted. But that was business.

"So, what do I tell Lara?"

"You believe that she will check out?"

Clay nodded.

"Then what reason could there be for telling her anything?" Sushma spun on her heels and left.

How does this stuff get so complicated? Clay tightened the towel again and headed back into the bedroom.

* * *

The fun evaporated from the fashion session after Sushma's appearance. Chartre kept throwing things around the room and tugging and pulling on Lara, but Lara focused on what might happen next. What if they know about Gina and *HardCoreGrrrls?*

When Clay returned, Lara studied his face. "Is everything all right?"

"Of course," he said, putting his hands on her waist. "Why wouldn't it be?"

He kissed her, right in front of Chartre and the assistants.

Chartre tapped his foot and drummed his fingers until he couldn't take it anymore. "You know, some of us wage slaves might be interested in taking a few minutes off on The Lord's Day."

Clay ignored him. "Are you okay with these new developments?"

"Do I have a choice?"

"Of course you have a choice. It's not company policy to force anyone to be in The Rotation."

"It's what we talked about last night, isn't it?"

"Chartre, give us a minute, will you?"

"Always the same: Hurry up and wait." He snapped his fingers and the assistants followed him out of the room.

Clay took Lara's hands in his. "Sushma's kind of—how do I say this? Suspicious."

"Ya think?"

Clay chuckled. "She's done a lot of work, so it's understandable that she'd be overprotective of the company. After you and I were seen together, the media got all revved up, and she thought she had to do something."

"Sun Tzu. She wants me close so she can keep an eye on me."

"Can you handle that?"

"Why wouldn't I?"

"That's exactly what I said." Clay smiled. "I have to go back to Hollywood to take care of some apparently urgent business. They'll keep you pretty busy here for the rest of the day, but we'll see each other again tomorrow. Okay?"

"Sure. Yeah, that sounds fine. Great, actually."

Clay kissed her and started collecting his clothes. "Don't let anyone or anything get under your skin. Just keep reminding yourself it's all good."

Lara and Clay kissed again, but before they were

finished, Chartre came back into the room and har-rumphed. "I assume the business part of this meeting is over?"

Clay slapped Chartre on the arm on his way out and gave Lara one last golden-eyed smile.

Chartre snapped his fingers, and the assistants came back into the room. Chartre pointed at a rack of clothes and said, "That one." The redheaded assistant handed a top to Chartre, and he held it up to Lara's torso. The neckline consisted of heavy silver rings that resembled a dog collar.

* * *

Three hours later, Lara wrapped a big, fuzzy robe around herself and flopped onto the bed. Who would've thought trying on clothes and shoes could be so exhausting? The mountain of clothes was so tall and dense it muted the sound of the waterfall.

Lara's mind spun like a wheel, bouncing from Clay to Sushma to The Rotation to her mission. She had known Clay for less than a week, but they had already shared some amazing moments, as though they were genuinely connecting. On the other hand, getting into The Rotation seemed way too easy. She shoved some clothes aside to let the tranquil murmur of the water work its magic. In no time, she was floating in a pool of warm comfort.

A knock on the door put an end to that. Lara

tripped over shoes as she groggily made her way to the outer suite. She opened the door to a perky nineteen-year-old who resembled a blond Lhasa apso with pink highlights wearing a miniskirted candy striper outfit, bejeweled flip-flops and nerd glasses.

"Hi," the candy striper chirped in a voice so cute Lara want to pinch its cheeks, "I'm Tiffany, and Ms. V said I'm supposed to escort you to your meeting."

"I'm having a meeting?"

"One sec." Tiffany checked a text on her phone and said, "Okay. That makes more sense. I'm also supposed to tell you about the meeting."

"What is this meeting about?"

"Oh, I wouldn't know that. I'm just a, you know, gofer and all."

"Can you tell me who it's with?"

Tiffany shrugged.

"When it is?"

"Yeah. They told me that." Tiffany nodded, but said nothing more.

"Well?"

"Oh—you want me to say."

Lara nodded.

"Um, right now."

"Right now?"

"That's cool, right? I mean, if you already had your phone, and everything, I guess they could have just called you."

"My phone?"

"Everyone at Fast Lane gets a phone. An excellent one." Tiffany held up her company-issued phone. It was ensconced in a fuzzy aquamarine leopard-print case that made it look like a high-tech Muppet.

"Nice case," Lara said.

"You can get, like, a million different cases so you can match them with your outfits. I mean, if you're that kind of person."

"An animal print with stripes?"

"I'm not that kind of person."

"I see." Lara watched Tiffany come into the room and look around. "I have to get dressed now."

"Cool."

Lara moved back into the bedroom to look for something to wear. She didn't expect Tiffany to follow her to the mountain of clothes.

Okay..."Do you have *any* idea what the meeting is supposed to be about?"

"I'm just a—"

"Gofer, I know."

"Actually, I'm an intern. Maybe they just want to give you your phone."

That helps.

"OMG! They gave you the DK!" Tiffany ripped a sequin-covered tank top from the middle of the pile, held it up to her scrawny torso and checked herself out in the mirrored glass wall. "Completely boss!"

140

"I should wear *that* to the meeting?"

"Tae-Q totally would. But she's, like, 'If there's a rule, I'm breaking it.'"

"Tae-Q?"

Tiffany looked embarrassed. "Taequanda lets me call her that. But, you know, only when no one else can hear. It's, like, a between-girls thing, you know?"

"I do."

"So, you won't tell her?"

"Tell her what?" Lara smiled.

The guilty look left Tiffany's face.

"I don't know if I'm like 'if there's a rule, I'm breaking it,'" Lara said as she rescued a staid pencil skirt and a soft white button-down blouse from the pile. "These are more my style. What do you think?"

Tiffany put down the tank, walked up close to Lara, pushed her glasses to the end of her nose and leaned way back. "It's kind of, you know—briefcase-y. For a Sunday afternoon, I mean."

"How about this?" Lara said, holding up a black washed silk sundress with an African-influenced beaded neckline.

Tiffany nodded her approval. "With the Latin sandals."

"These?" Lara nudged a pair of flat sandals with a large black silk flower adorning the leather upper strap.

"Those rule." Tiffany slipped out of one flip-flop

and held her bare foot next to the sandal. "They totally go, dontcha think?"

Lara nodded. "So, I'll be getting dressed now."

"Cool." Tiffany continued rummaging through Lara's new clothes.

"Could you, maybe, wait for me out in the other room?"

Tiffany kept rummaging. "I'm good."

Lara thought about pressing the issue, then decided it wasn't worth it. *Maybe having people watching you get dressed and undressed is part of the corporate culture.* She slipped into the bathroom, got dressed and emerged a few minutes later.

"How do I look?"

"Excellent. Way excellent. Let's rock."

"Almost." Lara peered at the glass wall and tried to straighten out her hair.

"You don't have to do that," Tiffany said. "Your hair looks awesome."

"It's been through the wringer," Lara protested.

"Just do this." Tiffany pushed the hair off Lara's forehead.

Lara scowled and quickly pushed it back. "You're right. It looks good enough." Tiffany recoiled. Lara softened her tone. "After all, it's Sunday afternoon. Lead the way."

So Tiffany led the way down the hall, onto an elevator and past the front desk to a door Tiffany opened with a wave of her phone. Lara couldn't take her eyes off the burnished bronze "Employees Only" plaque on the door as she passed over the threshold from what her life had been for thirty-two years to whatever it was about to become.

TEN

*T*he door led into a long corridor lined with offices and conference rooms.

"Third door from the right." Tiffany bounded ahead, parked in the doorway and smiled.

Being herded again.

Lara stopped short of the door, her heart racing, palms sweating. The latter was bad. A telltale sign of lying.

"Don't worry." Tiffany's wide eyes gleamed through the cascade of silky hair hanging over her face. "You'll kill."

The girl's confidence was infectious. Lara wiped her hands on her skirt, straightened her back, took a deep breath and proceeded into the room.

Three people—two women and a man—huddled around a desk, looking over a stack of papers. One woman was about Lara's age, the other in her mid-twenties. The man looked about fifty and was the epitome of distinguished. All three wore suits.

Uh-oh.

The woman who was Lara's age looked up and smiled.

"Miss Dixon, I'm Candy Kane," she said as she walked toward Lara, "lead counsel for Fast Lane Enterprises."

"Candy Kane?" Lara hadn't recognized her, but the name stuck out from the list of former members of The Rotation. As they shook hands, Lara tried to connect the name to the photo she'd seen.

"My father thought that was a good idea."

"Oh, no," Lara said, sensing a need to cover up a faux pas. She did not want to make Fast Lane's top lawyer uncomfortable. "I didn't mean—"

"No worries. My dad's name was Dick, but everyone called him 'Sugar.' He always said no one could dislike someone with a nickname, so he cut right to the chase with me."

Her smile was so warm and welcoming that Lara could feel her blood pressure ease down a notch.

"Lara, Rafael del Lago. Meilani Ma'atupu."

Lara shook their hands, too.

"Rafe is V.P. of corporate communications; Meilani's in charge of new media."

"I'm sure it's been a whirlwind for you," Rafe said reassuringly. "To have so much thrown at you so fast must certainly be a little daunting."

A little?

"I'm sure it is." Candy had one mode—business-like. "But Mr. Creighton wanted to make sure certain formalities were taken care of right away."

Mr. Creighton wanted? Of course Lara had set out to be in The Rotation, but a part of her hoped Clay had other ideas.

Candy continued. "Anyway, what we need to do today is fairly perfunctory. Standard procedure for any girl who joins The Rotation."

Gina had warned Lara that women entering The Rotation would likely have to sign a nondisclosure agreement. She felt pretty sure of this because thirty-eight women had passed through The Rotation without any of them writing one word about it except for sycophantic guest spots on Clay's blogs. "What are the odds of that?" Gina had said with a sneer.

Even though she was prepared for what was about to happen, Lara worried about reneging on a signed contract. Gina assured her that HardCoreGrrrls would pay for her defense and let Lara retain the book and movie rights that would inevitably come her way. Still, Lara dreaded the moment when she would have to put the pen to the paper.

"Please, have a seat." Candy motioned them all to a C-shaped pit group in the corner of the room.

Lara sat in the middle as Tiffany brought in a

pitcher of jasmine-scented iced green tea and a set of the hand-painted hula-dancer tumblers that Lara recognized from the ICE House.

"So, Rafe," Candy said, filling the tumblers, "would you like to begin?"

A slight man, Rafe had a big presence. Maybe it was his broad shoulders. Or his impeccable attire. Or his shiny, slicked-back, dark, curly hair.

"We're not going to get it all done today, obviously," he said, "but we're going to be spending a considerable amount of time together developing your brand."

"I have a brand?"

Lara knew that whatever "the girls of The Rotation" were like in real life, precious little of it showed through in their public personas. "They have people whose job is to craft a personality for each woman that fits the Fast Lane 'mystique,'" Gina had said. "When they ask you about yourself, just tell them about your life. There's too much chance of stumbling over details if you make stuff up." Lara didn't think her life had been interesting enough for Fast Lane, but Gina said her movie industry background and knowledge of auto racing would provide plenty of grist for the highly paid corporate spin doctors. One thing was sure about Clay Creighton's consorts: None of them were dull.

"You don't have a brand yet." Rafe put a hand on

Lara's knee. *Doesn't anyone here respect personal boundaries?* "We know a little about you already—your previous marriage, your career in the film industry."

"I just wrote publicity pieces for my husband's—my ex-husband's—production company. I didn't even get paid."

"Ah, but you see, that is something we can use. You're a team player. Loyal. That kind of devotion is hard to find these days."

I was more like a towel boy, but it sounds better than saying a conniving son-of-a-bitch profited from my ignorance while fucking every two-bit, size double-D slut in the San Fernando Valley.

"So that's what we're going to do first." Lara found Rafe's confidence reassuring. "Brainstorming. Riffing, more or less, on...whatever. Your experiences. Your likes and dislikes. Your childhood. Hobbies. Favorite music. Dark secrets."

His eyebrows rose and he moved in toward Lara when he said "dark secrets."

"Dark secrets?"

"That kind of thing."

Lara nodded.

"I'll be in on those discussions, too," Meilani interjected.

"Yes, she will be in on the discussions." Rafe sighed and took his hand off Lara's knee.

Meilani focused on Lara. "You'll have your own blog, of course, and a Facebook page. And you'll be tweeting two or three times a day. More, if you like."

"Sounds like I'll be busy."

"Oh, don't worry—my staff will take care of all that. We just need to know where you're coming from."

"Your staff will write my blog and tweets?"

"Oh, yes. They're very good."

"When it comes to *new* media." Rafe straightened his tie.

"So, you two work together?" Lara asked.

"Actually—" Meilani began. Rafe cut her off.

"To a degree. *My* staff will develop the overall Lara Dixon marketing plan."

Meilani looked at Rafe with her eyelids at half-mast.

Candy jumped in. "Okay, so that's something you have to look forward to, Lara. We have more immediate business to conduct."

She stood and moved to her desk. "I know you two won't mind," she said without looking at Meilani and Rafe. They got up and left.

"I'm sorry you had to see that." Candy poured herself another glass of iced tea. "While we try to maintain a familial corporate culture at Fast Lane, ego sometimes infects matters. Rafe's never been happy Sushma created a separate department to handle new media, much less hiring a twenty-three-year-old to run it."

"I can see that."

Candy checked something on her phone. "Do you think you'll have a hard time working with a twenty-three-year-old?"

"Why would I?"

"Your age is kind of a delicate issue."

"There is nothing delicate about it at all," Sushma said as she strode into the room. "It is, in fact, very straightforward: The women in Clay's Rotation have always been much younger."

"*Much* younger? How old do you think I am?"

"We know exactly how old you are." Sushma poured herself a glass of tea.

"We?"

"Our researchers."

"If you wanted to know my age, you could've just asked."

"The average age of the previous girls was twenty-two and four months," Sushma said.

"And they all got along with the new media coordinator?"

"Touché." Candy put her phone down.

"Are we dueling?" Lara responded to Candy, but looked at Sushma.

"Events of the last week have been highly un-usual," Sushma said. "There is no precedent for the way you came to be in The Rotation, and that sends up a number of red flags at the corporate level."

"Maybe it's just a sign that Clay's growing up," Lara said. "He is, after all, thirty-nine years old. A man might be satisfied with twenty-two-year-old girls when he's twenty-two, or even thirty-two, I suppose. But he's—"

"You have made your point," Sushma interrupted. "And it could very well be a good one. Still."

"Still, I didn't ask to be in The Rotation."

"Not directly, no," Sushma said. "But you are saying the thought never entered your mind?"

Lara hesitated. *Walking on thin ice.* "Look, I know who Clay is. Who doesn't? But when Anton invited me to the party in Malibu, I thought, 'Okay, I'll go to see what it's like.' I might never get another chance."

All eyes in the room moved to Sushma.

"You never had chances like these when you worked in the motion picture industry?" Sushma said.

"You know what kind of movies my ex made. It's not like I hobnobbed with Brad and Angelina."

"If it's all right," Candy said forcefully, "I'd like to get this other stuff taken care of. It's not my place to judge what, if anything, is going on between you and Mr. Creighton. I just need these documents signed." She took three stacks of documents bound by metal clips from a folder and laid them out neatly, side-by-side. "Do you have an agent?"

"An agent?"

"Most of the girls who enter The Rotation either

have an agent or hire one," Sushma said. "If you don't know any, I can suggest a few."

"No." Lara shot Sushma an icy look. "I can do this right now."

Candy handed her a pen. A really nice pen. Sleek and perfectly weighted. Ignoring Sushma, Lara scanned the top document, then put the pen on the dotted line and signed her name in one bold stroke.

* * *

When Lara finally got back to the Oasis, the waterfall sounded like a thousand angels sent to drown out the noise of the day. Someone had hung her new clothes in the closet, so Lara sat at the edge of the bed and looked over her copies of the papers she'd signed with such furious intent.

One said Lara did not have representation and was acting as her own agent. Another bound her to wear clothes and shoes from merchants that had merchandising deals with Fast Lane. Another, to attend events Fast Lane scheduled for her.

Lara also had to acknowledge that she understood she would be receiving a stipend instead of a salary. Gina had prepared her for this. "They're going to say it's a stipend and not a salary because paying women to fuck Clay Creighton would piss some people off— including a few in the district attorney's office."

And then came the nondisclosure agreement. A sheet of paper, nothing more. And yet Lara kept staring at it. She had come in believing she would disclose the truth about Clay Creighton. But the better she got to know him, the less sure she was about the truth. *How could a man who could treats a woman so well be associated with something like The Rotation?*

Then again, Kyle had seemed like a pretty good guy. For a while.

Lara put down the papers and massaged her temples. *Maybe it's not too late to call the whole thing off with Gina.*

Lara's phone rang. It was Gina.

"Can you talk?" Gina asked in hushed tones.

"Yes. I'm alone."

"It's all over the Internet that you're in The Rotation," Gina said, still whispering.

"You can talk normally."

"You totally rock, girl," Gina said so loudly that Lara had to move the phone away from her ear. "You *totally* rock!"

"I do?"

"Getting in was the hard part. Now all you have to do is hang around and wait to see things almost no one gets to see."

"Yeah. Pretty cool. I've been thinking..."

"Uh-oh. I hear ellipses."

"You hear *what*?"

"That hitch in your voice says doubt's creeping in. Do *not* let it happen. Do not permit yourself to start any sentence with 'I've been thinking dot, dot, dot,' or 'it's just that dot, dot, dot,' or '*anything* dot, dot, dot' when you're talking to me—or anyone else. You got that?"

Lara stood and walked to the glass wall. It had been pitch black the night before. Mysteriously, invitingly dark. Now a pool party was in full swing. Topless women and bottomless margaritas and men with rippling pecs batting beach balls into the air like lottery balls in a see-through tank. Lara's eyes followed the balls without really seeing them.

"Lara?"

"It's just that—"

"What did I just say?"

Lara paused. "I'm not so sure Clay is what I thought he was."

"Of course you're not sure. That's part of his game."

"But—"

"He manipulates women—and he makes his living teaching men the tricks of his trade. You said so yourself."

Lara looked blankly out the window as a particularly well-endowed blonde on the diving board, a goddess who already lacked the upper half of what was, according to her tan lines, an itsy-bitsy, teeny-weeny bikini, slipped off the bottom and snapped it like a rubber band to a group of slobbering males in the water below.

"I signed all the papers," Lara said.

"Good. Then everything's still on track?"

Lara opened her mouth to reply, but stopped as the blonde turned to wiggle her bare backside, causing her worshippers to thrash spastically in waves of foam. A spiky-haired man wearing nothing but skin appeared on the board and struck a Scarface pose. Lara didn't have to be a lip-reader to know he shouted, no doubt with Al Pacino brio, "Say hello to my little friend," which he then graciously pointed out for anyone who might be oblivious to his cleverness. He cupped his hands in front of his crotch to approximate a large-caliber rifle and proceeded to shoot at the blonde, who, much to the delight of the faithful, grabbed the place on her chest where the bullets would supposedly have entered, then took a header into the frenzy below.

"Lara, remember: Clay Creighton's a—"

Lara turned away from the window. "Don't worry, Gina. Everything's still on track."

"That's my grrrl," Gina said. "Keep fighting the good fight. Call whenever you think you need to. Remember, I'm behind you. Me and umpteen million women. We all want you to succeed."

Lara hung up and sat back down at the edge of the bed.

She stared into the waterfall's veil of mist and thought about how telling her life story to the marketing gurus was more grueling and invasive than she could have imagined, about how signing the papers had made her intentions seem even more underhanded. She approached the cascade and stuck out her arm. The water felt welcoming and warm, as if it could wash away her doubts and fears.

The phone rang again. Clay. Seeing his name on the screen made her heart flutter. *Just like a seventh-grader getting a call from a boy in biology class—again!*

"Hey," she said. She couldn't help sounding tired.

"I understand you had a big day."

"Your people certainly know how to keep a girl busy."

"They're *your* people now, too, you know."

Lara hadn't really thought of it like that, especially since no one seemed to be on her side. "So what've you been up to all this time?"

"I had to take care of some things at the Rev office, then they whisked me over to the ICE House."

Lara wished she were at Clay's love pad, on the bluff where she could hear the ocean and breathe in the salt air. And feel Clay's arms around her. "Is that where you are now?"

"Yeah. I'd rather be in P.S. with you, but Sushma's worried about all the things that have to get done tomorrow."

"I've been filled in on the schedule."

"It's not all that bad. We hook up at eleven."

"Hook up?"

Clay laughed. "I didn't mean—it's just that, there's a photo shoot—" He paused. "You know, we could try to sneak off."

Lara laughed. *My god, he's acting like a middle-schooler, too.* "We could. Think about it, I mean."

"Yeah, we could. Think about it."

Lara bit her lip through a long silence.

"In the meantime," Clay finally said, "how 'bout I hang up and you turn off your phone and get a good night's sleep?"

"Sounds like a plan."

"It's going to be hectic the next few days," he said. "Just remember, I'm behind you."

"Great."

The room was again quiet except for the rushing water. Heeding its siren call, she turned off her phone, stripped off her clothes and let the water work its rejuvenating magic.

ELEVEN

*L*ara slept dead to the world, buried in the heavenly featherbed, when she swore she heard a bird peep. Directly into her ear. Her eyes blinked open to someone—bending over her!

And peeping!

An explosion of adrenaline blasted her out of bed. Lara shook as she struggled to maintain her footing and figure out what the hell was going on.

"Oh! Miss D! I'm so sorry." Tiffany's voice came from the floor on the other side of the bed. Her head popped into view, a deer-in-headlights look on her face.

"What are you doing here?" Lara clutched a giant, overstuffed bed pillow to her body like a shield.

Tiffany climbed back to her feet, clutching her phone to her chest. The candy striper look was gone, replaced with a hipster vibe that included a day-glo pink romper customized with hand-painted skulls.

"I did not mean to scare you," she said. "Really. I'm really, really, *really* sorry."

"Okay, apology accepted. Now tell me why you're here at—" Lara looked around, but couldn't see her phone or a clock. "What time is it?"

"Five-thirty." Tiffany sounded a little sheepish, and a little perky. *How is that even possible?*

"In the morning?"

"Yes."

"*Five*-thirty."

"Ms. V said she talked to you about today's schedule."

Lara's arms ached from holding the pillow so tight. As she put it down, she thanked her lucky stars she had decided not to sleep in the nude. "I remember talking about the schedule, just not anything about getting up at five-thirty."

Tiffany pulled the phone away from her chest and scanned the screen. "We're scheduled to take Elway to the Malibu house for a series of shoots with the other girls, then it's—"

"Wait."

Tiffany stopped and looked at Lara expectantly.

"Two questions."

"Okay."

"Actually, it's more like three questions, since you never answered my first."

"Okay."

"Elway?"

"The Rotation's helicopter."

Right. Fast Lane owned four helicopters, each named after a famed NFL quarterback: Favre, Montana, Brady and Elway. In his blogs, Clay referred to trips in them as "air strikes" or "going long."

"Oh, *Elway*," Lara said. "Like the quarterback."

"Wow—you follow football?"

"Kind of," Lara lied. "Everyone knows Elway." *I think.*

They blinked at each other, Tiffany wide-eyed and waiting, Lara with sleep still tugging on her lids.

"So," Lara finally said, "what else?"

"Um...you said there were more questions?"

"Oh, right. You said 'we' are going to be flying to Malibu."

"That's right."

"We?"

"Well, yeah. I mean, that would make sense, right?" Tiffany nodded.

Lara flicked her tongue behind her bottom front teeth.

"Oh!" Tiffany said. "I thought Ms. V told you."

Lara waited a moment for the rest, then said, "Told me what?"

"I'm your P.A. now."

Lara did the tongue thing again.

"Your personal assistant? On account of how we hit it off the other day?"

"The other day being yesterday?"

Tiffany nodded with exuberance, her Lhasa apso hair bobbing all around her face.

"I guess that explains a lot. But why did you wake me up at five-thirty?"

"Oh, well, you see," Tiffany moved briskly to Lara's side of the bed while manipulating the phone's touch screen, "I saw that you like to work out every day, and, really, this is the only time you'll have for that today. So I thought you might—" She froze when she noticed Lara looking down with a furrowed brow and pursed lips. "That's cool, right, Miss D?"

"What?"

"That I woke you up so you could work out."

"Huh?" Lara stared at Tiffany's legs until Tiffany looked down at her silver spray-painted army boots and tattered fence-net pantyhose that ended just above her knees.

"What, the pantyhose?"

And the boots. Lara nodded.

"I just snipped them off with a scissors." Tiffany tugged at the ragged tops. "And sewed in some elastic so they'd stay up. They're boss, right?"

"They're different."

"Thank you. That's so sweet. Is there anything else for now?"

"No, I think I'm fine."

"Cool. See you L eight R, Miss D." Tiffany bounced toward the door.

"Tiffany?"

"L eight R, like when people text and they mean 'later.'"

"I got that. Why do you keep calling me 'Miss D'?"

"You don't like it?"

"No, it's fine. It's just that no one ever called me that."

"Oh. It's what people do around here."

"So I should call you Miss T?"

"Oh, no. Definitely not. I'm not, like, a personage."

"A personage?"

"You know. Like you and Ms. V and Mr. C."

"So, what should I call you?"

"Tiffany."

"Right." Lara smiled. "It was cool to wake me up at five-thirty so I could work out. Very good thinking."

Tiffany let out a sigh of relief.

"But," Lara continued, "is there any time in the schedule for me to get a little breakfast?"

* * *

Breakfast was a short stack of whole grain pancakes done exactly the way Lara liked them—crispy around the edges, pleasantly spongy in the middle—served with a medley of fruit, including the biggest, sweetest blackberries Lara had ever seen or tasted. The gym had all the latest equipment and a massage therapist named Gretchen who gave Lara a vigorous rubdown in a steam bath fit for a Roman palace. Everything at Heat, like everything associated with Fast Lane, was top-notch.

Afterward, Lara showered in the waterfall. Tiffany helped her pick out "traveling clothes," a simple black shift and comfy sandals. Two of Chartre's assistants packed the rest of Lara's mountain of new clothes onto the helicopter. Tiffany assured Lara that anything else she might need or want would be available at the ICE House.

Lara and her new girl Friday boarded Elway at eight forty-five. Twenty minutes into the flight, Lara looked out a window and marveled at the way humans had managed to colonize every nook and cranny of the Los Angeles basin. Even the slopes and tops of those mountains that bisected it all were crisscrossed with roads—roads that Lara, lamentably, had so seldom taken advantage of. She wondered how many people there were like her who felt alone in the midst of an almost endless cityscape. Had clinging to Van Nuys been a shrinking violet's way of avoiding novelty and adventure?

Van Nuys. I wish. When's the last time I told someone I grew up in Reseda?

"It's amazing, isn't it, how spread out it is?" Tiffany looked through the window over Lara's shoulder. "It's so great, though, how easy it is to, you know, just hop onto the freeway and live whatever dream you feel like having that day. Your bio says you're from the valley?"

"I grew up in Van Nuys," Lara said.

"That is so awesome."

Van Nuys is better than Reseda. But awesome?

"When I was in high school," Tiffany chirruped, "my friends and I would just drive until we saw something cool. One time we hit this unbelievable farmers market in Encino that had all these wild veggies and things, like kohlrabi and champagne grapes and this spicy Vietnamese paste that we didn't even know what you were supposed to do with it, and we ordered these unbelievable fish tacos. Sometimes we'd randomly stop at some restaurant—they have the best Mexican restaurants in the valley. Authentic. Not like the bullshit ones on the West Side."

"You don't like any restaurants on the West Side?"

Tiffany shrugged. "Some. But the valley is, like, *real*, you know?"

"I've been to the farmers market you're talking about," Lara said. "Never tried the fish tacos. Which restaurant do you mean?"

"It was...si. Si something."

"Si Maria?"

"Is that a real restaurant?"

"Yes."

"Then, no. It was more like solly."

"Sol y Luna?"

"That's it! Wow!"

"I must've eaten there a hundred times growing up."

"Get out!"

"They have the best chili rellenos."

"Are they like heaven?" Tiffany gazed off into the ether.

Lara nodded.

"I had a combo platter, because, you know, that way, you can try lots of different things," Tiffany said.

"Where did you grow up?"

"Silver Lake."

"But you hung out in the valley?"

"I hung out everywhere. Hollywood. Korea Town. Tarzana. I mean, there's so many awesome places. Not like I have to tell *you*." She sat in the seat next to Lara and checked her phone. "I'm totally stoked that we're talking like, you know, BFFs, but there's still some business to cover. It's cool, right? To talk business?"

"We don't have to hate each other to talk business."

"Oh, right. That's awesome, because we'll be in Malibu in ten."

Tiffany went over the schedule again. Lara tried to pay attention, but she figured the schedule would change and people would herd her around all day, so there was no reason to memorize anything. Instead, she thought about how much Tiffany's view of the world differed from her own. If she had approached life with that much gusto, might she never have gotten mixed up with her asshole ex-husband? And was it possible that, instead of being on a mission to avenge the wronged women of the world, she would be happily married somewhere? Or working as a publicist for A-list stars who made A-list movies?

What would I be doing right now? Not flying into Malibu to meet a bunch of people whose livelihood I'm secretly trying to destroy.

* * *

As the chopper approached its destination, Lara marveled at the size of the ICE House compound. The house jutted from the cliff, leaving plenty of room for tennis, basketball and jai alai courts, a pool, a smattering of spas and a serpentine dirt track that ran in and around and through everything else.

"Sometimes Mr. C and other people get into these little go-kart things and race them around the track," Tiffany explained. "And that massive building over there? That's where he keeps all his totally boss old cars."

"Wow." Lara wasn't thinking about go-karts or

antique cars. She was thinking about selling her ruse, starting with the two incumbents of The Rotation. *What if Taequanda and Corynne don't like me? What if they can tell I'm a fraud?*

"So," Tiffany said, "are you nervous about today?"

Oh, shit, she can tell. But wouldn't anyone be nervous in my position?

"Should I be?"

"Not really. I mean, anyone would. But you're going to like the other girls. And they're going to like you."

"That's reassuring." *Truly*.

"Then there's Spike."

"What is Spike? A guard dog?"

"The photog. He does look like a dog, though."

"A mean one?"

"A snippy one. That likes biting your pants leg."

"I see," Lara said, though she didn't really.

Elway touched down.

"He'll probably take like a million shots of you right as we get off the copter," Tiffany warned. "He'll expect you to look natural, like you're not even aware that he's there, so don't try to look glamorous or whatnot."

Lara nodded. "Gotcha. Look natural."

"Just be you." Tiffany said. The chopper's doors flew open.

The first thing Lara saw was the piercing flash of a camera. The first thing she heard was a high-pitched, somewhat male, sing-song voice blaring, "Gotch-aaaaa!"

Lara blinked away the flash to see a hedge of silver hair. Not gray. Not white. *Silver.* The singsong voice came out of a mouth below a pair of glasses with the thickest, blackest rims Lara had ever seen, and it said, "I lu-uv that. Every new girl...always the same!"

"Now I know what you mean about Spike." Lara had to talk over the roar of the engine and beating of the blades. She moved forward, but Tiffany grabbed her arm until an assistant put down a step.

"A little to the left," Tiffany said into Lara's ear.

One instance where I don't mind being herded.

"Spike, you are such a fucking asshole," said a statuesque black woman with angled cheekbones and sumptuous purple lips. She held out her hand and smiled at Lara. "Take my hand, honey. I'm Taequanda."

She wore a dress similar to Lara's, but while Lara could feel where hers tugged and bunched, Taequanda's looked and moved like it was part of her body.

"I'm Lara."

"Everyone knows who *you* are," Corynne said as she put an arm around Lara's waist. "I'm Corynne."

The experienced Rotation members flanked Lara and guided her toward the house. With the flashes and the sun and the Santa Anas blowing her hair into her face, Lara worked hard to appear natural. The other two, on the other hand, simply looked natural. *Such poise.*

"Okay-yee!" Spike wailed. "Let's get inside, pee-pull! Grande-double-latte to do today!"

Lara screwed up her face. *What?*

"What he's saying is he's a pompous ass," Taequanda said. "Hey, Spike—how about talking in a language familiar to humans?"

Lara winced as Spike unexpectedly snapped a shot just inches from her face. No matter where she looked, she saw nothing but purple dots.

"That should look natural," she said.

"Don't let his bullshit get to you," Taequanda said as she and Corynne led Lara to the door. "Don't let any of this bullshit get to you."

* * *

Inside hummed like a beehive. Assistants worshipping their phones and gaffers and grips lugging poles and dollies and lamps danced in a frenzied ballet up and down the halls and into and out of the various rooms.

"How many rooms does this place have?" Lara asked.

"Sixty-nine," Corynne said.

"Sixty—?"

"You got it," Taequanda chimed in, shaking her head. "That's what happens when men get a say in things."

"It looks like we're having our pictures taken in every one of them." Lara dodged a grunt who raced down the hall with a stack of boxes.

Taequanda glared at the grunt. "Hey!"

The grunt stopped cold and looked around the boxes at Taequanda. "Sorry."

"Damn right, you are." She turned to Lara. "Everybody knows that kind of thing doesn't fly with Tae-Q."

"Girlfriends!" Spike's annoying soprano surfed above the clamor. He clapped twice. The crowd parted and he sailed toward the three women.

He looks like a Disney character. Aladdin, but with spiky metal hair.

"I know what you're thinking," Corynne said. "He's a bit over-the-top, but he actually knows what he's doing."

"Just don't ever let him think you think he does," Taequanda said.

Spike stopped a few feet away, put his hands on his hips, leaned back and gave them the once-over. Multiple times. "My, but are-ent *oui* altogether a vision of eeee-ternity!"

Lara's eyes narrowed as she tried to figure out what he meant, why he had said "we" like *oui* but with an H in front of it so it sounded like "hwee." *And why does every sentence he says seem to end in an exclamation point?*

"Can the flattery," Taequanda said. "We know we're too hot for the Mojave. But we're here to work."

"Oh, that you are," Spike said, eyeing Taequanda head to toe. "And, baby, I love to watch you work!"

He winked at Lara, then turned on his heels and sped away, throwing an arm in the air and pointing ahead.

"That means he expects us to follow," Taequanda explained.

"He's quite a..."

"Yes he is."

"Just don't let him cop a feel when he's supposed to be positioning you," Corynne added.

"*He's* going to cop a feel?"

Taequanda and Corynne looked at each other and laughed.

"Whatever it may seem like, Spike likes tail," Taequanda said. "The feminine variety."

Lara must have looked confused, because Taequanda put an arm around her in sisterly fashion. "I know, it's like *Alice in Wonderland* around here," she said. "Nothing is the way you think it should be, so just chill and take it all in. We'll run interference for you."

Taequanda and Corynne did a hand-bump and held it, signaling with their eyes for Lara to join them.

"The 'girlfriends' got to stick together," Taequanda said.

* * *

The three trailed Spike into a room decorated as a Roman dining hall, with reclining benches surrounding a large central table piled high with brightly colored fake food.

"The hell is this?" Taequanda said.

"I thought it would be fun to go with a salacious bacchanal theme," Spike said. "After all, you are a feast."

"I feel like chocolate cookie dough in a tube squeezed into this instrument of torture." Taequanda tugged on her dress.

"Don't worry, sweetheart," Spike reached out to touch Taequanda, but she grabbed his wrist and looked at him with one eyebrow raised before letting go. "As I was saying: We'll start with formal shots, then come back here for some fun, then do the swimsuit shots on the rocks. *Va bene?*"

He did another about-face, put his hand over his head again, snapped his fingers and forged ahead.

"Aren't we going to have a session with Clay?" Lara asked, too late for Spike to hear.

"There will be a session with Clay when the time comes for a session with Clay," Sushma said from just behind Lara.

How does she do that? Lara whipped around. "Oh, I didn't see—"

"Tiffany," Sushma said. Lara had almost forgotten about Tiffany. Like everyone else around here, though, the girl had the ability to materialize out of thin air.

"Yes, Ms. V."

"I believe I said Miss Dixon was to wear the Chan Luu."

"Yes, right. I suggested it, like you said, but she tried it on and decided the Love Moschino was…"

She mumbled the last words.

"I am sorry?"

"More comfortable?"

"I hope that's not a problem," Lara said.

Sushma eyed her like a displeased schoolmarm. "As difficult as it is for me to believe that either dress would be uncomfortable, the point is for you to look good and to appear to be comfortable. Whether you *are* comfortable is not an issue."

I see.

"Chartre picked out both dresses, did he not?"

"Yes."

"Then both dresses are equally comfortable."

Sushma turned to Tiffany. "When I ask for Chan Luu, I expect to see Chan Luu."

174

"Yes, ma'am."

"It's not her fault—" Lara began, but Sushma had already turned on her five-inch heels and vanished into the crowd.

Lara looked at Tiffany. Tiffany looked at the floor.

"I'm sorry," Lara said. "I'll tell her later it wasn't your fault."

"I should have been more emphatic about which dress you were supposed to wear," Tiffany countered.

"Can you tell the difference between this dress and the other one?"

"Totally. I mean, this one is a little longer in through here," Tiffany ran her hands down her own hips, "and smoothing along here." She clenched her own waist.

"So, this *was* the wrong choice?"

"Oh, no!" Tiffany looked around, then put her face up to Lara's ear. "You have a great figure, and this one does a way more excellent job of showing it off. I mean—OMG, you won't tell Ms. V *that*?"

"No. Strictly a between-girls thing."

"If neither of you tell her, I sure will." Taequanda nodded vigorously. "Oh, yeah. That dress is having its lucky day. It never looked as good as it does right now."

"Thanks, both of you."

"Don't thank us. Thank the all-knowing Lady who rules from on high—and I do not mean Ms. V. Plus the fact that you're obviously well-acquainted with Mr. Arman Curl." Taequanda pumped her arms.

Lara smiled. *Looking natural sure is a lot of work.*

* * *

It became even more work when Lara, Taequanda and Corynne were supposed to pose as patricians lounging around in stolas as they enjoyed a sumptuous feast of faux food. Lara just couldn't get comfortable. The generous folds and pleats of her garment kept getting stuck underneath her.

Spike sighed conspicuously and let his camera drop into the hands of a dutiful assistant.

"I'm sorry," Lara said. "It's just that—I don't know."

"Oh, my god, girlfriend," he said, "this is not rocket science. All you have to do is sit there and look gorgeous."

I'm not stupid—I've just never done any modeling.

"Excuse me?" Taequanda had not said spoken loudly, but the room went dead quiet.

"I wasn't talking to you, Q." The look in Spike's eyes said he knew he was walking on eggs.

Taequanda looked down and calmly plucked a loose thread from the neck of her toga. "As you know," she said, "it is my policy that when you're talking to one of us, you're talking to all three."

Then she looked at him. With eyelids at half-mast.

"Oh, come on," he said with a self-conscious giggle. "There's no reason to get your panties in a bunch."

The three people standing closest to him each took a step back.

"My *what*?"

Everyone else in the room took a step back.

"You're talking about my what? My panties? How about let's have a little conversation about the ones *you're* wearing?"

"How about, why don't we just proceed?"

"Oh, I do not think so." Taequanda stood up on the reclining bench and scowled. "Before we do anything, you need to give 'em a tug here and there."

"I beg your par—"

"You heard me: A tug here and there. Give your junk a little breathing room."

"I really don't understand what—"

"That's right, you don't understand. You know that girl's never done anything like this before."

Not wanting to make waves, Lara sat up and offered, "Thanks, but it's all right. Really. I just have to get used to—"

"You ever do any modeling before today?"

"No."

"Then it is *not* all right."

Taequanda glowered at the assembled multitude. "In fact, it's all wrong. I have never in my life seen so many people with their shorts on so tight." She softened her expression and turned to Lara. "Seriously, I've never seen these people so wound up." The glower returned as she turned back to the crowd. "Now, I want everyone—and that would include you two"—she pointed at two assistants who were still conversing at the back of the room—"to loosen their shorts."

Everyone stood still, blinking at the tall, dark, majestic woman towering over them in glowing white, flowing robes.

"Do I have to demonstrate for you people?" She hiked up her stola, whisked her underwear down to her ankles and kicked them right at Spike.

Lara surveyed the shocked faces. *Thank god they're all looking at Taequanda instead of me.* Then she noticed Corynne looking down and covering her face, trying not to let everyone see how hard she was laughing.

"Come on! Loose shorts all around!"

Spike sighed as he took Taequanda's underwear off his shoulder and nervously flexed the waistband between his index fingers.

"Tae, dear," Spike said, "I think you've quite made your point."

Taequanda's arms were crossed now. "You all had better hope so. Because if I don't start feeling a more relaxed vibe *tout de suite*, some asses will get kicked."

After a moment of silence and trepidation, Spike twirled his arm above his head. "Everyone take two to chill."

The buzz returned to the room, but at a much lower decibel level. Corynne stopped trying to hide her laughter. Taequanda, though, was all business as she turned to Lara.

"You know it's *their* job to make you look comfortable even if you feel like you've got lobsters pinching on your eyelids."

"It's just that, every time I tried to put something up to my mouth, I felt this...thing...tugging me or sliding off my body."

"Let me show you a secret." Taequanda lifted one side of her toga before sitting on the bench.

"See how it just ends up in the right place?" The material seemed to cooperate no matter how she moved her head and shoulders and arms, even when she reclined into the traditional Roman dining position.

Lara copied Taequanda's trick and got the same results.

"How could it be that easy? I feel so dumb."

"It's not you. They just throw you into these situations and expect you to perform." She turned toward Spike, who was talking to an assistant. "Hey! Annie Leibovitz—shake a leg!"

Spike stopped midsentence and looked at her.

"That's right. I said you may continue."

He snapped his fingers. "People, her highness, the queen, wishes for us to get on with it."

The entourage snapped into gear like a machine.

"Around this place," Taequanda said to Lara, but loud enough for everyone to hear, "you are a queen. It's *their* business to make you look good, not the other way around."

TWELVE

*C*aequanda's advice helped ease things for Lara as the day wore on. Spike took shots of the girls in the kitchen. Shots of them playing pool. Shots of them goofing off in the backseat of one of Clay's massive Pierce-Arrows. A Jacuzzi shot was planned, but when Lara confided her aversion to hot tubs, Taequanda asked Spike—politely, and with her underwear in place—to skip it.

The next shot still, however, required wearing a swimsuit. Trim though she was, Lara found picking a swimsuit stressful. Tiffany laid out a half-dozen choices, all of them black one-pieces.

"Which do you think?" Lara bit a thumbnail as Tiffany scrutinized each suit.

"I couldn't totally say unless I saw you in each one. But, I don't see how you could go wrong, since Chartre picked them out."

"Chartre picked them out?"

Tiffany nodded.

"Then, which one would Ms. V pick?"

"Definitely not this one." Tiffany pointed to an Amalfi bandeau. "This one, for sure." She held up an Athena Maldives "fauxkini." Lara snatched up the Amalfi.

Lara felt fine about going strapless, but when she saw her Rotation mates on the rocks below the War Room, she thanked her lucky stars the bandeau covered her hips. Not afraid to reveal all her assets, Corynne had chosen a tankini with a plunging neckline from Victoria's Secret. Taequanda, of course, looked the best of the three in a Monica Wise suit with side cutouts that Lara would dream of wearing only in a nightmare.

Wranglers kept sunbathing seals at bay as the trio posed on boulders that were as big as some houses in the neighborhood where Lara grew up. The sun felt warm, but every now and then a wave smacked the rocks and launched plumes of chilly spray that made Lara shiver. *Lucky seals. No one cares if they have enough blubber to keep them warm.*

At the end of the shoot, as the Rotation mates' respective assistants appeared with fuzzy pink robes, Spike stopped in front of Lara and nodded. "I have to admit," he said, "you *do* know how to wear a swimsuit."

Lara smiled demurely. "Thank you."

Tiffany held the gigantic robe up to allow Lara to peel off the freezing swimsuit. As soon as the spandex hit the rock, Tiffany wrapped the robe around Lara the way a fight trainer would a boxer. The terry cloth tickled her skin, and she warmed up immediately.

Clay never showed. But Lara, feeling the need to play it cool, didn't ask why. Instead, she dutifully followed Tiffany to her own space in the ICE House, a suite that overlooked the ocean from two flights above the deck.

* * *

"Here ya go!" Tiffany said as she threw open the double doors.

The ante room was bigger than Lara's entire apartment at Eleventh and Pearl—and much nicer. The décor was feminine but not effete, functional but comfortable. And even with its infinite view of the ocean, it seemed cozy. Lara thought the radiant hardwood flooring and plush oriental carpet had something to do with that.

Lara checked out the spacious bathroom. "No waterfall?"

"I hope that's not going to be a problem. The shower is totally boss, though." Tiffany danced out of view.

Lara followed her through a dressing room big enough for two people to live in. Chartre's mountain of clothes had been neatly hung and obsessively arranged by occasion and color in a huge walk-in closet. Lara stopped and stared.

All this is mine?

Lara heard the shower go on. Still staring at the clothes, she headed toward the bathroom but stumbled over something in the doorway: Tiffany's boots. Tiffany's shredded stockings lay on the tile just inside the bathroom. Lara looked up to see her barefoot assistant marveling over a glass-encased stall big enough to hold three, or maybe four, people.

"You can make it do all kinds of wild things by turning this knob," Tiffany said gleefully. As she rotated the control, jets of water shot out of the walls from various angles.

Lara stuck her arm into the stream. Tiffany turned the knob to make the water pulse. "As good as a waterfall, for sure," Tiffany said. She turned off the water and scooped up her boots and hose.

"I hope you don't mind me taking them off," she said without guilt. "I just love the way the natural stone feels on bare feet."

They moved back into the bedroom. Lara stared at the comically high pile of pillows burying the bed. "Are there enough pillows?"

"Why? Do you want more?" Tiffany tucked her boots and hose under one arm and typed a note on her phone.

"I was being facetious."

"Oh." Tiffany stopped typing. "Because, I can get you more pillows."

"No. These will be fine."

Tiffany shrugged and put her phone away. "So, the room is cool?"

"I like it very much."

Tiffany picked up a remote from one of the night-stands. "Well, in two seconds, you're going to like it to death."

She clicked a button and the blinds opened to a sunset coloring the steel-green canvas of the sea incandescent oranges and pinks.

With the touch of another button, she made the glass door open. "Voilá! Your own private deck."

Deck?

Each sunset gave Lara a deeper appreciation of the romantic appeal of the city she had lived in all her life. And she had wondered why that romance had so often seemed to be so maddeningly out of reach. She went onto the deck and stood mesmerized. Many times in the past two years she had watched the sun set from the top of the bluffs over Santa Monica Bay, staying until the last dazzling rays shone like a halo over Point Dume. Malibu. *And, now, me.*

"Pretty decent, no?" Tiffany brushed the smooth wood of the deck with her feet.

"It's just like in the song," Lara said.

"There's a song about a deck?"

"No. The sunset."

Tiffany joined Lara at the railing.

"The Doors song, *L.A. Woman.*"

"The Doors? Were they on Jimmy Fallon last week?"

Lara laughed. "I don't think so. There's a verse about how a woman's hair looks like hills on fire, like she's standing in front of a sunset."

"I can totally see that."

They stood in silence for a few moments and watched the explosion of color.

"Okay, so, I'm supposed to ask if there's anything you want brought here from your place in S.M."

"What?"

"Ms. V said it's cool. All the girls do it."

"That's nice, but I don't think—"

"It's not like you'll *need* anything. But maybe you'd like to, you know, personalize the space. Maybe you have some beloved clothes? Or a favorite snuggly?"

"Snuggly?"

"A teddy bear or a dog. Or a big, cushy walrus with googly eyes. Like that."

"A big, cushy walrus with googly eyes?"

Tiffany nodded. "Like that."

Lara turned back to the sunset. "There's so much here...I don't think I'm going to miss anything back in 'S.M.' for a few months."

"Or, like, your laptop? I could arrange to have someone pick it up for you."

My laptop? It does have my research on it. But the last thing I need is anyone from Fast Lane...

"That won't be necessary."

"Are you sure? Because it's no—"

Lara spun around. "I don't need it."

It surprised even Lara how bitchy she sounded, but paranoia was spreading through her like an infection. Could all these compliments and banter about "snugglies" be Tiffany trying to lull her into a false sense of security? Why did Taequanda always take her side? *Sushma has me second-guessing everyone.*

"Okay, cool." Tiffany poked at her phone. "So, tomorrow, you can sleep in to, like, eight, if you want, and still have time for a workout and breakfast."

Tiffany's nonchalance made Lara feel even more off-balance.

"Um, okay."

"Cool."

Lara forced a smile. "Cool."

Tiffany floated toward the door.

"Oh, and Tiffany?"

"Yes?"

"Tomorrow, could you please wake me up by calling me on my phone?"

"Gotcha, Miss D."

* * *

Alone, Lara became aware of how big a silence could be in the wake of a hurricane. Still, the exchange with Tiffany and *L.A. Woman* buzzed in her mind.

Am I a lucky lady? Or lost in a city of light?

The last ember of sun glowed the color of the sparkle in Clay's eyes. Lara leaned against the railing and looked at the rocks so far below. The water now lapped lazily against the bluff.

Her phone rang.

Why at a moment like this? Lara thought about letting the call go, then went inside to answer it.

It was Clay.

"Hi."

"How was your day?"

"Kind of hectic. Yours?"

"Kind of hectic."

"I'm guessing your days are always hectic," Lara said.

"I never showed up during the photo shoots."

I noticed." Lara tried to sound more inquisitive than disappointed.

"Like you said: Things come up when you run a major business enterprise."

"But if *you're* the one running the enterprise, don't *you* get to say when the plans change?"

"Sure, but..." Clay paused. "I delegate."

"You have people tell you where you should go and when you should go there?" Lara went back onto the deck so she could watch the colors fade from the sky.

"Frees me up to think about more important things."

"Such as?"

"You."

"Ha! How often did you do that?"

"Just about, oh, once a minute."

Lara batted her eyelashes. "And what, specifically, were you thinking once every minute?"

"I was wondering, 'How's Lara doing on her own with all those sharks?'"

How many sharks? "You mean Spike? He's more of a guppy."

"You had Taequanda on your side."

Gulp. "Someone told you?"

"No one told me anything. Those two are so predictable, like an old married couple. He practically begged to have his ass kicked, and she was happy to oblige. Am I right?"

"That's a pretty dim view of marriage."

"Why? Don't we all need someone who's happy to kick our ass, keep us honest?"

Lara laughed self-consciously and brushed the luxurious pile of the robe with her free hand.

"Spike's a good photog," Clay continued, "but he's also a fool, and Taequanda does not suffer fools gladly."

"Thank god for that."

"Anyway, like your new digs?"

"What's not to like?"

"How 'bout the deck?"

"Great place to hang with Sol," Lara said with a sigh.

"Sol?"

"Watch a sunset. Sorry."

"No, 'hanging with Sol.' I like that. Malibu is the greatest place to hang with Sol."

"I don't know about that. I like where I usually go."

"Where do you usually go?"

"Ocean and Arizona."

"It *is* nice there. So how would you improve the view from your deck?"

Lara looked toward the corner of the sky where the light had faded to deep red with purple edges that blended into the gathering blackness. "Maybe if you moved the sun a little to the left."

"I could talk to someone about that."

"So you do have clout around here."

"On the other hand," Clay continued, "my view might improve if *you* moved a little to your left."

"What?"

"Just a step."

Lara looked left, then right, then turned around.

"Perfect!" Clay said. "Reminds me of the first time I saw you on the Upper Deck, standing at the railing."

"Wait. Where—?"

"Up here."

Lara looked up to see a leg swinging from a dormer a few feet above her deck. Clay was perched on the roof wearing an ear-to-ear grin. He slipped his phone into a pocket and slid forward, deftly landing in front of Lara.

"How long were you..."

Pushing aside a few stay strands of hair, his eyes were ablaze with desire. "Long enough to realize you're the only thing in the world that could improve a sunset."

Lara snapped her phone shut. Clay cradled her chin and kissed her.

* * *

Lara felt the blood rush from her head as Clay's tongue danced ever so lightly across hers. Her shoulders went limp, and the rest of her followed. Clay put his hand on her waist and pulled her close. Their breathing became synchronized. Their bodies melded.

Only forty-eight hours had passed since they'd made love in the waterfall at Heat, but with all that had happened in those hours, it seemed like a lifetime ago. The pace of the day had been physically demanding and emotionally grueling, with constant reminders of how she was faking it. Of how far in over her head she was. Of how wrong she had been about Clay. Lara's body and soul focused on the immediacy of his presence; her mind kept jetting forward to a time when she would have to get out of the hole she was still digging.

That time could be now. She could break off this kiss and confess everything. *Clay would understand. He would want to help me. He would help me. Or maybe he'd have me shipped back to "S.M."*

Or Sushma would. No matter what, confessing to Clay would put an end to Lara's Big Plan. Would that be so bad? What earth-shaking revelations had she dredged up? Spike personified the most egregious gay stereotypes, but was a closet hetero lecher with wandering hands. Heat hosted naked pool parties for young, beautiful people. Women in The Rotation didn't write their own tweets. Clay wasn't really in charge. *All firmly between "ho" and "hum" on the Richter scale.*

When their lips separated, Lara kept her eyes closed. It kept the moment alive—but Lara also feared that if Clay looked into them, he would detect her deceit.

Lara turned toward the water. "Clay, why didn't you just knock on my door?"

"This feels naughtier." He hugged her from behind and whispered, "It drives them crazy when they can't find me."

"You're playing hooky from work?"

"To spend time with my favorite girl." He nibbled on her ear.

Lara closed her eyes. This was one of the sexiest men in the world. A cultured man. An arbiter of sensibilities. A man who could make a woman feel she was the only woman who ever lived—and mean it. Sure, he had flaws. Who didn't? But who was Lara Dixon? A boring girl from the valley whose life's résumé contained not much more than a community college degree, a failed marriage and a partially hatched plan to save the world from—what?

What does he see in me?

"Clay."

"Shhh."

"What did Anton Roche tell you about me?"

"Anton Roche?"

"He said he'd mentioned me to you and you wanted to meet me." Lara turned to face Clay. "What did he tell you?"

"He said you knew about racing. That you'd worked in the movie industry. That you were bright and funny. And sexy. He said you were the—how did he say it? 'The aurora borealis, Liberty's torch and the leprechaun's pot o' gold rolled into one.'"

Lara laughed.

"What?"

"Was he telling the truth?"

"I haven't seen any evidence to the contrary." Clay brushed the hair off her forehead. She bobbed her head to knock it back into place, but when it didn't cooperate, she decided to let it go.

"Clay, I—" she began, but he put a finger to her lips, then swept her into his arms and carried her inside to the bed. He kissed his way from her lips to the base of her neck. Lara felt that melting sensation return.

Clay untied the robe and reached inside. The feathery fabric felt cushy against Lara's flesh, but Clay's caresses were heavenly—and then some. He slid his palms upward from her stomach, slipping around the edges of her breasts and around the curve of her shoulders. Lara pulled Clay's shirt off over his head and tossed it wantonly out into the room, then pushed back her robe's terry cloth lapels. Clay's eyes widened at the sight of her bare torso. Starting where he had left off, he continued kissing his way down her body.

When Clay got to where the robe was still closed, he buried his face in the pink nap and continued on his way. Lara sighed when Clay finally pushed the dense fabric to each side and parted her legs. Starting at her knees, he stroked her thighs with his clean-shaven chin. He then teased her with his breath, warming her folds. Lara moaned and arched her back as Clay slowly worked his tongue inside her until she was ready to explode. She did not want to climax this way, though. She wanted him inside her. So she ran her fingers through his hair and, when he looked up, guided his face to hers. They kissed, and Lara tugged on his waistband.

"It can't be very comfortable having these still on," she said. Clay stood, and Lara unhitched his belt, pulled down the zipper and let his pants drop to the floor. Clay was already hard, and she stroked him through his plain white briefs. *Vanilla underwear on a man of so many flavors.*

"How's that?" she asked.

"Nice."

"And how's this?" She leaned forward and nibbled through the pima.

Clay closed his eyes and took a deep breath.

"And this?" Lara ran her index fingers along the inside of the elastic band and peeled off the briefs.

Clay answered with a lascivious smile as he sat on the edge of the bed, opened a drawer in the nightstand, took out a condom and ripped open the package.

"Allow me." Lara snagged the condom from Clay and took her sweet time sliding it into place, unrolling it partway and letting her cupped hand slip the last few inches, then cocking her head to evaluate her progress. Clay played with her hair the whole time.

"There," Lara finally said, admiring her handiwork.

Clay pushed her back into a reclining position. Strange though the surroundings still were to Lara, the weight of his body felt familiar. Like something she always had known. Something that always was meant to have been.

When he was inside her, all of her doubts and concerns disappeared. Nothing else mattered. Nothing else even existed. The ocean, infinite and so near, vanished. The strain of the day was swept away by soothing caresses. Painful memories and fears of inadequacy floated away in the effervescence of the moment.

* * *

Half an hour later, Lara lay on her back with Clay snuggled alongside her, asleep, head on her chest, breathing rhythmically and low. Lara remained awake, her eyes trying to penetrate the deep shadows. Her mind worked in overdrive, trying to undo a tangle of thoughts, worries and emotions. *How can the best and the worst be happening at once?*

And then she noticed the blinking "missed call" light on her phone. *Like I need another thing to worry about. I'll check it in the morning.*

She closed her eyes and tried to will herself to sleep. But they shot open just a few seconds later. *What if Clay wakes up and sees something I can't explain?*

Lara moved one arm deliberately toward the

nightstand, trying not to disturb Clay. She panicked each time he breathed, certain he was waking up. After what seemed like an eternity, she finally reached the phone. She picked it up and, craning her neck, saw Gina's name and number. Paranoia shot through every nerve. Gina Wray was a well-known presence on the web.

And a sworn enemy of Fast Lane.

She carefully worked the flip-phone open with one hand and tried turning it off, but it slipped and hit the glossy blond wood of the nightstand with a clunk before tumbling to the floor.

Clay's head popped up. "What...?"

"Nothing," Lara said. She guided his head back down. "It's a beautiful night. Let's just sleep."

She stroked Clay's hair as he nestled into a comfortable position and fell back to sleep. Lara remained awake far into the night.

THIRTEEN

*Y*ou had better hope you find him before I do,"
Sushma snarled into her phone. Her voice
was as cold and murderous as a gunfighter's as she
charged from her office.

"Yes, ma'am," came back the cool, confident voice
of Morgan Hopkins, the man who'd headed security
at the ICE House since Chase Creighton built it in
1968. "Where do you suggest we start?"

"Never mind. I will take care of it."

"Let me know if you change your mind." He was
well acquainted with Sushma in shark mode.

Sushma marched up to Lara's suite and pounded
out a code on the number pad. The door clicked
opened.

"Where is he?" Sushma barked as she entered the
bedroom.

Lara yelped as she jolted awake.

"Where is he?"

He? Lara blinked and ran her tongue around her dry mouth as her body and brain trudged up to speed.

"Where is Clayton?" Sushma's voice came from the dressing room.

Clay? He left.

Lara scooched up to a sitting position, clasping the sheet in front of her. Unlike the previous night, she had not put anything on before falling to sleep; she had wanted to feel Clay's skin touching hers. "Doesn't *anyone* around here knock?"

"It is seven twenty-five. Clayton was supposed to be in my office at seven fifteen." Sushma stormed back into the bedroom, stood at the foot of the bed with her hands on her hips and glared at Lara.

"Satisfied?" Lara hissed.

"You do not fool me."

"You've looked everywhere but under the bed! Here, let me help you." She leaned over and yanked up the dust ruffle. Something caught her eye.

My phone! Fuck! Now Lara was fully awake. *Keep cool.*

Lara let the ruffle drop and looked back at Sushma with steely eyes.

Sushma straightened her suit jacket, smoothed the skirt and folded her arms. "You cannot play your little games with me."

"Games?"

"You are attempting to make me make a fool of myself."

Lara just cocked her head, daring Sushma to look.

Sushma ground her teeth; she clearly did not want to lose this bizarre game of chicken.

They were interrupted by a knock on the open door.

"Hello?" Morgan called. "Everything all right in here?"

"You are the chief of security; why do you not see for yourself?" Sushma called back, keeping her eyes on Lara.

"Someone said they heard something funny, so we came right away." Morgan entered the bedroom, trailed by two young male assistants. When he saw Lara, he matter-of-factly looked away, but the assistants had a hard time keeping their eyes in their sockets.

"What is their problem?" Sushma demanded.

Morgan turned to the assistants.

"She's not wearing any clothes," one assistant babbled.

"I'm glad somebody noticed." Lara hiked the sheet all the way to her neck.

"I apologize, ma'am." Morgan nodded without looking at Lara. And then, like a Zen master to two incorrigible pupils, he addressed the assistants. "What a professional does in a situation like this, gentlemen, is simply avert his eyes."

He waited for a moment, but the assistants were intractable. "Never mind. Go wait in the hall."

"Both of us, sir?"

"Yes, both of you." Morgan grabbed their arms and escorted them to the door. They kept sneaking peeks at Lara until he closed the door in their faces.

"Now," he said, "I believe this young lady and I have not been properly introduced."

Lara extended her hand. "I'm Lara Dixon."

"Nice to meet you, Miss Dixon." Morgan looked at her eyes as he shook her hand. "I'm Morgan Hopkins, chief of security here at the ICE House."

"Nice to meet you, Mor—"

Sushma interrupted. "Oh, for heaven's sake. Do your job."

"Yes, ma'am. What would you like me to do?"

"Help me locate Mr. Creighton."

"Yes, ma'am. Have you checked the bathroom?"

"Of course. Look under the bed."

"Yes, ma'am."

Shit.

Morgan dropped to his hands and knees, peered under the bed and felt around.

"All clear," he announced as he climbed back to his feet.

Lara's heart skipped a beat when she saw Morgan holding her phone—with the "missed call" light still blinking. "I believe you dropped this, Miss Dixon." He put the phone on the nightstand. Face-down.

Whew. "Thanks."

"Shall I continue the search, Ms. V?"

"Yes. And when you find Mr. Creighton, inform him that I am not pleased that he missed our scheduled meeting."

Morgan headed for the door, still careful not to look in Lara's direction.

"Mr. Hopkins?" Lara said, smiling. "Thank you for respecting my privacy."

"Of course, ma'am. Let me know if you ever need any help from me or my people."

* * *

Lara's smile vanished as she turned to Sushma. "So, are you planning to look around a little more?"

"Your sarcasm is unbecoming. I have a few things to say."

"Could I put on a robe or something?"

"By all means." Sushma crossed her arms and waited.

"Could you at least turn around?"

"Oh, for Christ's sake." Sushma pursed her lips, sighed and turned grudgingly around.

Lara retrieved the pink fuzzy robe from the floor, where it had ended up the night before. "Why did you think you would find Clay in here?"

"Do not try to act coy. I know he was here."

"Is there a rule against that?"

"No, there is no 'rule.'"

"Then what is your problem?"

"May I turn around? Your highness?"

"By all means."

Sushma turned around. "*You* are the problem."

"Why would you say that?"

"I have my reasons."

"Do you treat every woman who comes into Clay's life this way?"

"Do you know why you are here today? Why you have been brought into The Rotation?"

"Because of the way Clay and I—" Lara stopped herself.

"The way you and Clay what?"

Lara went into the bathroom and squeezed a generous helping of toothpaste onto a brush. "The way Clay and I have hit it off since meeting a week ago?" She swished the toothbrush around in her mouth.

Sushma appeared in the doorway. "For the record," she said, "I do not believe you are a stupid person."

"High praise," Lara sputtered through the foam.

"I assume you know by now that Clay Creighton does not choose the women who join The Rotation."

It was hard to miss.

Lara spat out the toothpaste. "So?"

"The Rotation is a business proposition, Miss Dixon. An extremely important business proposition. Every dollar Fast Lane earns proceeds from it. And it so happens that Clay Creighton—the man millions of men depend on for advice about women—is a particularly poor judge in these matters."

Lara's jaw stiffened. "*Business* matters, you mean?"

"Precisely. When it comes to business, he makes appallingly bad choices."

"If I'm such an appallingly bad *business* choice, then why *did* you bring me into The Rotation?"

Sushma got right up into Lara's freshly polished grille. "I have brought you into The Rotation so that I can keep my eye on you."

"I see. If Clay were allowed to date me—or whatever—on his own, anything could happen, including"—she moved so close to Sushma that their noses almost touched—"the end of The Rotation."

Sushma's gaze hardened from steel to titanium. "Everything you do for the next several months—every minute of every hour of every day—comes under the purview of Fast Lane Enterprises Incorporated. If you were interested in 'privacy,' you should not have signed the agreements. Do we have an understanding?"

Lara nodded coolly.

Sushma strode out of the room.

Lara remained rooted in place until she heard the door slam. She looked in the mirror and saw she still gripped her toothbrush tight. Like a dagger. She put it down and went into the bedroom, where the first thing she saw was her phone.

Gina.

Shit.

Lara picked up the phone and stared at Gina's number. Lara thought about calling her back at that moment, but then turned the phone off and set it back on the nightstand.

She needed to think.

* * *

Not one hour earlier, Clay had awakened from a particularly restful slumber and lain next to Lara for a good half-hour. He didn't want to pull some kind of clichéd one-night-stand move by leaving, but he was never going to fall back to sleep. Not with so many thoughts crashing about in his brain. Lara breathed slowly next to him, her skin softened by the lanolin effect of sleep. Clay turned his face to smell her hair. A moment of perfection. He wanted it to last forever, and the only way he could think of making that happen was to get up and start getting dressed before anything happened to change it.

Lara turned over and smiled at him sleepily.

Clay kissed her forehead. She ran the back of her hand along his face and chin. He liked how smooth it felt against the bristle of his unshaven skin.

"What time is it?" Lara asked.

"Six-twenty."

"You always this eager to greet the day?"

"Why wouldn't I be?" he said, his eyes gleaming. "Life is good."

"It's not so bad hunkered down in between these silk sheets, either." Lara pulled up the covers and rolled onto her side.

Clay considered the contours of her body. Smooth. Curvy. Alluring. But he had to go. People would be looking for him.

"I have to talk to someone," he said.

"At six-twenty?"

"He doesn't live in this time zone."

Clay brushed Lara's hip with his hand as he started toward the deck. His toe bumped something on the floor, but he couldn't see anything, so he headed outside.

Fog lingered as Clay climbed onto the roof. He passed the steps that led to the War Room, dropped to a sandy hillock topped with tall, swaying grass and marched toward the building where he kept his antique cars.

It was a defunct Packard dealership, a quaint edifice that Chase had transplanted brick by brick from Mendocino a half-century before. As Clay entered the showroom, he drew a deep breath to savor the cocktail of smells: Rubber and oil blended with carnauba wax and a dash of old leather. *Not a bad place for a man to live out eternity.*

He strolled past the massive, chrome-covered beasts of the 1950s—a Hudson Hawk, a Nash Ambassador, two Buicks, a Ford—and continued around the cartoonish balloon-fendered cars of the '40s toward the sleek, art-deco masterpieces of the '30s that had led Chase Creighton to an epiphany about how an ideal woman would look. "The curvaceous architecture of a '36 Delahaye," he famously wrote in the inaugural issue of Fast Lane, "is sex set in steel. Behind the wheel, a man is not merely driving a car, but having an erotic experience nonpareil."

Of course he had not meant to equate driving to being with a woman. But Fast Lane readers understood. Clay did, too; Chase's prized jet-black and silver Delahaye reminded him of Lara under the sheets. He smiled and continued on, past the twin brown-over-gold '39 Bugatti Avaris to a '38 Buick that Chase dubbed "The Forever Mobile" because it looked so much like the car Cary Grant

and Constance Bennett are driving when their characters from *Topper* smack into a tree and enter the afterlife.

Clay stroked the edge of the distinctive tail fin and climbed in. The ancient leather seats creaked as they conformed to his body. He caressed the steering wheel and tugged on the shifter knob, then opened the glove box and took out its sole contents: a fading photo of Clay and his father sitting in this very seat on the day Clay turned sixteen. The two of them were off to the Simi Valley DMV so Clay could take the road test for his driver's license. Clay smiled, remembering the examiner's face when they pulled into the parking lot. The examiner had administered exams in a few Bentleys and Ferraris, but got quite a thrill from riding in a vehicle so rare.

Clay stared at the photo. He wanted to tell his father about what was happening in his life. About Lara. How she was different from every woman who had passed through The Rotation.

She's not interested in having her fifteen minutes of fame or jump-starting a career or whatever. This one's for real. She's interested in me.

"You'd like her, Dad."

He smiled again, this time at the thought of a Creighton man walking down the aisle. Chase had been intimate with an untold number of women until he met Clay's mom and transformed, overnight, into the consummate family guy. They never got married—too bourgeois, too conventional, too uncool, man, for the 1960s—but Chase remained faithful to her until, still pretty in spite of being ravaged by disease, she died on the morning Clay took his first step.

"And, hey," Clay said to the photo, "tell Mom I've

found someone who reminds me of what I think she was like."

He was about to slip the picture back into the glove box just as one of the big garage doors slid open.

"Good morning, Mr. C," Morgan said. "Am I interrupting something?"

"It's never an interruption if it's you," Clay answered. "Just having a moment to myself."

The older man took out a cloth and shined the Buick's stately hood ornament.

"Yeah," Morgan said. "I come here, too, when I want to spend a little time with your father."

He stepped back and admired the hood ornament over the top of his glasses. The chrome glinted in a shaft of sunlight.

"She sure is pretty," he said.

Clay nodded.

Morgan turned to leave.

"Morgan?"

"Yes, sir?"

"You were talking about the hood ornament, right?"

"I could've been." He winked and smiled. "Oh, and, I assume you know Ms. V is looking for you. What should I tell her?"

"Tell her to keep her panties on."

"No, sir, I don't think I will. I'm only seventy-two and still have a few good years ahead of me."

The two men smiled at each other.

"I'll be in her office in a few minutes."

"Yes, sir." He sauntered away.

Clay looked at the photo again, then put it back into the glove box.

* * *

Sushma had not been gone from Lara's room for more than two minutes when there was a knock on the door.

Finally, someone has some manners.

Lara opened the door to see Tiffany in a long-sleeved, red velvet minidress. One sleeve had been replaced with black lace, and chrome-plated cotter pins and rubber loops stood in for buttons.

"Interesting outfit," Lara said.

Tiffany bounced into the room. "The dress came from a thrift store in Venice. The sleeve I found on some lacy underwear in my grandma's old trunk. I guess she was kind of a naughty girl."

"So I can see."

"These," Tiffany said as she tugged on a cotter pin, "I picked up at Pep Boys."

"It's very nice."

"Thank you," Tiffany said in her birdlike sing-song. "Now, if you eat breakfast and work out in the next hour and fifteen minutes, you'll have plenty of time for your sit-down with Magda."

Tiffany punctuated her pronouncement with a tap on her phone.

"Magda."

"Your stylist?"

"I have my own stylist?"

"Technically, she's the stylist for all three of you. The girls in The Rotation, I mean. She needs to see you early today so she can do an evaluation."

Lara looked at her, waiting for more.

"You know: Face shape. Skin tone. Follicle analysis."

"Something to look forward to."

"Oh, no. Magda's totally boss. You'll like her. After she's done with the eval, she'll do your face and hair, and then it's time to make the intro video."

Ah, yes, the intro video. Lara had watched the intro videos of all the past new Rotation members.

"No worries," Tiffany continued. "I already worked here when Corynne did hers. They prep you and make it pretty clear what you should say—but not too clear, because it's supposed to sound, you know, real. And, of course, Mr. C will be there the whole time."

"Oh?" Though prepared, Lara felt a case of the butterflies coming on. Hearing Clay would be there made something else flutter inside her.

"Great," she said. "If Mr. C is there, what could go wrong?"

FOURTEEN

*T*he session with Magda turned out to be, as Tiffany predicted, totally boss. Magda stood barely five feet tall and had a round figure. Like a lot of women on the far side of seventy, she had big, coiffed hair. But unlike lots of women her age, she wore very little makeup—something Lara noticed only when Magda commented, in a grandmotherly Eastern European accent, "I am happy to see you are not gunk up your face."

"I've never been great at makeup. I really like what you've done."

"Ach, what I have done? Is right there already. All I do is bring out what is natural. You are having such nice shick bonns." She outlined Lara's cheek with her finger. "Now I ask: Why you are coloring over your pretty blond hairs?"

Lara felt a buzz of fear. Dyed hair—so easy for a

professional to spot. "I just wanted to...try something different," she lied.

"Ho, well. Will grow out again, so is no harm." Magda squinted and pointed to her temple. "But always remember: What is natural, that is the most beautiful."

Despite Magda's demonstrated abilities, Lara balked at having her hair up for the intro video. Up was how Lara wore her hair when she cleaned her oven or lumped around the apartment alone. Hair worn up was glamorous—for other women. *Women who have prettier foreheads.*

"I don't know," Lara protested. "It doesn't seem to be me."

"If not you, then who does it seem?"

"Let's just say I'd rather not."

"Why you would rather not?"

"I have kind of a big forehead."

"Ach. How can forehead be *big*? Is exactly right size, or you would be having different forehead."

Magda slung Lara's hair low, then swept it back up past her ears and swiveled the chair around so Lara could see.

Lara gently patted her new 'do, then retraced Magda's outline of her attractively highlighted shick bonns.

"Hair is ulleginn. Claasic. Everybody can see more of your pretty face."

"My father used to say that."

"A father always know true how beautiful his daughter."

Lara looked at Magda in the mirror. The elder woman nodded.

"And not just shick bonns and boops," Magda scolded, grabbing her ample breasts to accentuate her meaning. "A good father see into his daughter heart and soul. That is where the beauty."

Lara cringed.

"You make ice like you don belief? *All* good man see this tings. Not just father. Boyfrenn. Lover. Hussbin."

Magda's eyebrows arched high when she said that last one. Lara didn't know what to say next. Fortunately, Tiffany bubbled into the room. "They said I should come in and find out when Miss D will be ready."

"What do you ting?" Magda said, spinning Lara around.

"Wonderful," Tiffany said. "I like how—" She finished the thought by outlining her own cheeks. "I'll tell them any minute."

Lara got up to go.

"Now, you and your wonderful shick bonns and forehead...go and knock them for dead, yes?"

"Yes, I will. I *will* knock them for dead."

She hugged Magda, thcn headed into the studio, ready for her close-up.

* * *

Unfortunately, they weren't ready for Lara. The studio contained more equipment than any movie set she could remember from when she worked with Kyle. The décor, on the other hand, consisted of a king-sized bed buried under a mound of throw pillows in front of a curtain. A huge crystal vase on a nightstand overflowed with freshly cut honeysuckle, narcissus and foxglove.

A bedraggled assistant acting as Lara's placeholder sat uncomfortably on the bed. Spike, who today had pink hair—*What happened to the chrome?*—and was dressed like an undertaker from a spaghetti western, ordered another bedraggled assistant to move a spotlight imperceptibly back and forth. Each time he massaged his chin as he studied the results, and each time he shook his head before barking, "Left!" or "Right!" or "Toward China! No—San Dimas!"

"Hey, elegant hair." Corynne swiped a hand up and over her own forehead.

"Thanks. It was Magda's idea."

"Yeah, she's good at that whole 'finding the inner you' thing."

"Where's Taequanda?"

"She's not involved in this. The No. 2 girl always introduces the newbie."

Lara nodded politely. Though she had come to feel

at ease with Taequanda, she hadn't gotten to know Corynne at all. Corynne seemed to be more guarded than Taequanda. Then again, Lara had been guarded around Corynne.

"So, they got you all prepped?" Corynne asked.

"Prepped? Not really. Actually, not at all."

"Oh, wow. They had me spend a couple of hours with Spike and the corporate image people before we shot mine."

Right. And I'm going in cold. Lara's brow crinkled. *And my stupid forehead looks like a hairless shar-pei.*

"No worries, though." Corynne patted Lara's arm. "They probably think you're already good at this kind of thing because of your experience in the movie business."

"But I didn't work in front of the camera."

"Really? Huh. I guess I had a completely different impression."

In the credits, Lara had been Kyle's director of public relations. She did appear in several movies as an extra and doubled for blond actresses in back shots. The one time she got to face the camera, she stood so deep in shadows that no one could see her.

"*Moi, moi, moi,* but aren't we looking like a movie star?" Spike studied Lara's face, then leaned way back so he could scan her body, too. He tugged at the waist of Lara's black chemise, nodded approvingly, then lightly pinched her chin and moved her head up and down and from side to side.

"You've done something with..." He pointed to his own cheeks, then: "No, wait. More like..." He swiped his hand across his forehead.

"It was Magda's idea. You like it, right?"

He continued looking at Lara for an uncomfortably long time. "Yes, me do," he effused. "Me likey. A-lots."

He spun around again, made a wide, dramatic circle with one arm and announced, "Let's go, pee-pull!" and finished with three crisp claps.

* * *

"We have to take our places." Corynne took Lara's hand and led her to the bed. They climbed onto it and sat with their legs tucked under them. Spike played with the miscreant spotlight—the one trained on Lara—a little more, his constant clucks and frowns indicating he was having no better luck than before. The brightness stung Lara's eyes so that she did not see Sushma come up to the bed.

"I am pleased to see that everyone is so chipper today."

Lara squinted. "I'm glad to see you, too. Nobody's said anything about what I should talk about, and Corynne said—"

"The purpose of the video is to introduce you to the world. Your biography, so to speak."

"But wasn't someone supposed to prep me?"

"Are you not familiar with your own life story?"

The old cat-and-mouse game again.

"So, I should just talk about...me?"

"You should be able to handle that without needing to rehearse."

"Of course. I just want to make sure we're on the same page."

Sushma made a motion with her fingers and an assistant handed her a manila folder filled with papers.

"Perhaps this would help."

Lara slid out the first sheet and tried to make sense of what she was reading. The second page had more of the same. So did the third. And all the ones that followed.

"Who told you—" Lara could hear herself getting louder, so she paused to collect her wits before continuing more quietly. "Who told you all this?"

"You do not know?"

"Kyle."

"Does reading about these events disturb you?"

"What *events*? None of what it says here ever happened."

"In that case, you might *not* want to talk about them in your introduction video." Sushma snatched the file and marched away, leaving Lara with a dry mouth and sweaty palms.

"Okaaay, pee-pull, let's get rolling!" Spike clapped again. An assistant opened a door and Clay strode in. Lara took solace in his confidence—and in the thought of what was underneath his signature white cotton shirt.

As he got onto the bed, Clay said, "Yo, Spiker, ease up on the death ray."

He brought his sparkling golden-rimmed irises to within a few inches of Lara's. "Hey, babe. Like your hair. I can see more of your face."

Things are better already. She wiped her hands on the bedspread.

Clay squeezed Lara's shoulder as he nestled into the mountain of pillows. "Come back over this way a little," he said, patting the space between them. "You'll go blind over there." Lara started to move back—but Corynne moved faster, crawling in between Lara and Clay and kissing him on the cheek.

"Hey, Corr. Feeling kinda gung ho?" Clay's voice contained no hint of sarcasm or surprise. Lara, though, felt a flash of heat as Corynne arched her back and stuck her little twenty-three-year-old butt in the air.

Who does she think she is?

For some reason, at that moment, Lara noticed that Clay wore slippers. Expensive ones, for sure—they were Ugg Romeos—but still incongruous, considering the rest of his wardrobe.

Focus on what matters, damn it.

No matter how hard she tried, though, Corynne

mattered most. The peck on the cheek. The skanky crawl. The loose-fitting shirt. The way she avoided making eye contact.

"Okay-yee, we start with sweetie Corynne giving her spiel, then we turn it over to Mr. C." Spike raised his arms, making him look like a vulture in cowboy drag. He glanced around the silent room, smacked his hands to his sides and shouted, "Act-chee-own!"

"Hi, I'm Corynne McFee. I've been a member of The Rotation here at Fast Lane since February." Corynne's voice sounded lower and smokier, like a woman in an ad for a "local singles" phone line on late-night TV. "One of the great things about being involved with Clay and with living the Fast Lane life-style is that there are so many opportunities to get to know really amazing new people all the time."

She's already said Fast Lane twice! Do they be expect me to do that?

"You've probably already heard about the newest addition to the Fast Lane crew."

Three times!

"Her name is Lara Dixon, and she's really great. She's pretty and exciting and fun, and she's had a glamorous—and mysterious—career in the movie business. I'm sure she'll want to tell you all about that."

Wait a minute...

"You're going to just love her. I, myself, only got to

meet her just a couple of days ago, and already I feel we've known each other forever, like sisters."

What?

The butterflies in Lara's stomach morphed into crows. Her mind—and her heartbeat—raced as Spike signaled for Clay to talk.

"Thanks, Corynne," he started. "You know, all the girls in The Rotation are special to me."

Lara could tell he spoke with his usual bravado, but she couldn't make out most of the words over the cawing in her ears. She heard something like, "corra girlatation spesha," followed by a bunch of garble. The last syllables sounded like "wafferfall."

Wafferfall? He's not talking about us making love in the waterfall? Maybe if I look at him I'll be able to understand. She tried to turn her head, but the room moved instead. In slow motion. *I'm going so fast; why is everything else going so slow?* She saw Sushma, hands on hips, head shaking in obvious disapproval. Then she saw Corynne, eyes at half-mast, licking her lips and making circles on Clay's leg with her fingers.

She suddenly became aware of the scent of the foxglove. Movement off to one side caught her eye. Her head rotated at two miles per hour until she spotted Spike, crouching and pointing at her with both hands in the stance used by TV cops carrying gigantic handguns. His mouth moved as though his jaw had turned to liquid.

And there was no sound. The flowers next to the bed swayed as though they were underwater. *Like a fish in a bowl.*

Lara forced herself to turn toward Clay. He looked surprised. *Concerned?* His eyes still had that sparkle. It grew and spread until the whole world seemed to shimmer, as if Lara were looking through amber into a bright light.

And then, everything went black.

* * *

Lara's eyes flickered open. It took her a while to realize she lay on the bed in the studio with Clay cradling her head in his lap. The buzzing in her ears blended into the hubbub around her. The sun seemed to be beaming directly into her eyes, but Lara felt cold and sick to her stomach. The fishbowl effect was as strong as before. Eyes peered at her from every angle.

The world stopped spinning when she saw Clay's smile.

"Welcome back," he said.

"Wafferfall?" Lara's voice sounded shaky and thin. She tried to sit up, but she swooned with a moan. Clay caught her.

"Hey, whoa! There's no hurry," he said. "Just take it easy."

"He's right, honey," Corynne said. "Don't do anything rash."

Lara's vertigo returned when she moved her eyes to Corynne.

Clay addressed the room: "Has anyone called a doctor or 9-1-1 or anything?"

"I'm on it." A dutiful assistant whipped out his phone.

"A doctor?" Sushma interjected. "What would be the purpose? She merely fainted from the lights."

"Yeah, how 'bout that, Spike?" Clay said. "I told you to cut back on the candlepower. She's probably got sunstroke."

"Oh, dear," Spike said. He looked at Lara like she was the corpse at a funeral. "Oh dear, oh dear, oh dear."

"Spike," Clay said, "look at me."

Spike kept right on babbling.

"Spiker!"

Spike stopped and looked at Clay.

"Turn off the goddamned light!"

Spike stood frozen and muttering. A gaffer cut the switch.

"So, should I call 9-1-1 or not?" The assistant with the phone looked from Sushma to Clay.

"I'll be all right." Lara had to close her eyes to sit up. "I just need some air."

"Everyone out!" Clay commanded. "You're using

up all the air!" It was as take-charge as Lara had ever heard him be.

"I'm going to take that as a 'no.'" The assistant with the phone looked back as he followed everyone else out of the room.

Pretty soon, Lara and Clay were alone. Except for Sushma. Lara could focus now—enough to be able to detect not even a hint of compassion on Sushma's face.

"Um, Shush," Clay said, more sweetly than Lara thought Sushma deserved, "when I said 'everybody,' I meant *everybody*."

"As chief operating officer, I have every right to be here."

"I didn't say you didn't have the right." Clay didn't utter another word, but his puppy-dog eyes said *please* as clearly as if he had shouted it. Sushma glared at him, then huffed, turned abruptly and left.

* * *

Lara nestled against Clay with her head on his shoulder. He brushed her forehead with his other hand, following the line of her upswept hair.

"I don't think *that* was in the script," he said.

"There was a script?"

"You gave everyone a scare."

"Everyone? Even Sushma?"

Clay smiled.

Lara massaged her forehead. "She doesn't like me."

"Who says?"

"We've butted heads."

"She butts heads with everyone. It's her thing."

Not the way she butts heads with me. Lara looked down and saw Clay's slippers. "Why are you wearing slippers?"

Clay chuckled, but stopped when Lara's face remained serious. "No big deal," he shrugged. "Just part of the Fast Lane lifestyle. Be comfortable. It's one of the Cardinal Virtues."

"The Fast Lane lifestyle? You mean business as usual?"

"Well, yeah. What else?"

Lara pushed away from him, dropped her feet over the side of the bed and forced herself to stand. She was woozy, but managed to right herself before Clay sprang to his feet and grabbed her arms.

"Maybe we *should* call a doctor," he said. Lara could see genuine concern in his eyes.

"Right before I blacked out, I heard something like..." Lara looked Clay in the eye. "Am *I* 'business as usual'?"

Clay's face went blank.

"The War Room," Lara continued. "Rev. The salt flats. The waterfall. All business as usual?"

Clay's lower lip quivered. "Oh, no. Not at all. I

mean, now, here...the video, and all...yeah. But, there's business, and then there's..."

"What?"

"Um..."

Lara could feel Clay's hands get clammy. "Are *you* going to be all right?"

"I'm trying to think what to say." He looked around the empty studio. "What an idiot. I mean, I give men advice on...you know...things with women."

"Maybe you'd better sit down."

"No." Clay held Lara more firmly. She liked how strong and powerful he felt. Assured. Assuring. "No, you are *not* 'business as usual.'"

"I'm not?"

"I—I don't...You'd think I would know what to say."

I know what I want you to say.

Saying nothing, he pulled Lara to him and kissed her. Lara recognized it as a delay tactic, but she didn't resist; it made her heart beat faster and cleared the clouds from her mind.

The door opened and Tiffany fluttered in. "Um, Ms. V is wondering how Miss D is—oh! Oh!"

Tiffany turned away and held her hand up as a blinder. Lara and Clay looked like a couple of thirteen-year-olds caught necking.

"I'm fine, Tiffany," Lara said. "Tell Ms. V I'm ready whenever she is."

FIFTEEN

*T*he subsequent shooting of the intro video went smoothly. Lara talked about her life, which made her glad she and Gina had rejected the notion of concocting a designer past.

The designer past in Sushma's folder, though, still weighed on Lara's mind hours later as she stood on her deck, sipped wine and watched the sun sink behind Point Dume. While Kyle hadn't been big on love, he did have a fondness for kink. He especially liked sharing fantasies populated by real people. To please him, Lara made up stories about being with his friends or a pizza delivery guy. Kyle talked about actresses and set decorators he worked with. But Kyle's fantasies turned out to have contained more fact than fiction.

Kyle had told Sushma's investigators that Lara had "slaked her rapacious sexual appetites" by indulging in sexcapades with not only his friends and a pizza guy, but also his dickhead brother. *Kyle said "rapacious"?* Lara shuddered and cringed. Just the thought of sex with Drake Lobo turned her stomach. But a scumbag like Kyle understood lack of proof was no problem; gossip could be deadlier than actual indiscretions. No one expected the women of The Rotation to be virgins—hell, they were *supposed* to be experienced—but the notion of a slut who cheated on her husband *with his brother* would not fly in the Fast Lane universe. Once tagged to a man, a woman was supposed to keep her panties on tight unless *he* demanded otherwise.

If Sushma kicked me out of The Rotation, would I be off the hook with Gina? Would it matter? Lara gazed at the sky, but the colors were invisible. *No, I have to confront Sushma. In private. Make her see reason.*

Or, at least, challenge her to come up with more proof than just the word of that fucker Kyle.

Thinking of Gina reminded Lara of the voicemail message. She rested her wine glass on the railing and opened her phone.

"You are *not* going to believe this, but things just got a lot cooler." Gina sounded like a little girl at Christmas. "I got a major publisher to agree on a book deal, a long-form version of the article you're doing. We're talking seven figures. Seven fucking figures! They want all the dirt, and by all, I mean *all*. Names. Places. Pornographic details. So take good notes."

If things get any cooler, I'm going to die from the heat.

Heat. Lara thought about the waterfall. She could feel Clay's fingers massaging her hair.

"Hey." Clay's voice came from behind Lara as she snapped the phone shut. Jolted, she fumbled the damn thing to the deck and kicked it through the railing. It bounced onto the deck below, then skittered through that railing and plummeted so far she couldn't even hear it smack the rocks.

Lara looked over the railing, fruitlessly scanning the murky shadows of the jagged wave-washed terrain.

Clay sidled up next to her. "I'm sorry. That was my fault."

"Oh, well. Just a cheap, stupid phone."

"Could be a big deal to some people."

It could be a big deal to me. "I'm not really a big phone person," she said with a shrug.

She looked at Clay out of the corner of her eye. *Can he tell I'm trying to con him?* "I mean," she continued, "it's not like I can't live without it."

"Really?" Clay turned her to face him. "*Is* there something you can't live without?"

You take the lead.

Instead, he kissed her.

Nice, but not what I hoped for.

"It's been an amazing week," he said.

231

The understatement of the year.

He continued: "The night we met, did it even cross your mind that you might be living here? And so soon?"

That was the plan. "Life can be unpredictable."

"There've been women all my life..." Clay faltered.

"Yes?"

"I've been surrounded by sexy, smart, exciting women all my life." Another pause. "But you're not like the others."

"Oh?"

"In some ways you are. The part about being sexy, smart and exciting."

"I'm glad to hear that."

Clay hesitated again. "I think about you and—the company be damned."

"I see."

"I know. That sounds lame."

"No it doesn't."

"It doesn't?"

"No."

"What I mean is...what I want to say. Ah, here I go again."

Lara put a finger over his lips, then pulled him close and kissed him.

"We have all night to talk," she said. "For now..." She tugged on his arm, but he didn't move. He looked sheepish.

"What?"

"I can't stay here tonight. I have a previous commitment."

Lara frowned.

"And here I was just going on about 'the company be damned.'"

Lara tried to mask her disappointment. "Hey, it's a previous commitment. I understand."

"Tomorrow night," Clay said brightly. "I'm free then."

"No 'previous commitments'?"

"I just made one, didn't I?"

They kissed again, and then Clay scrambled up over the roof and disappeared into the night.

Lara went to the railing and gazed upon the moonlight shimmering on the water. She couldn't stop herself from looking again for the phone, but all she could see were blackness and foam. Not an ideal send-off to bed. But for now, she was comforted by the sound of the ocean in her ears and the taste of Clay on her lips.

* * *

Lara woke up early the next morning rested and ready to rumble. After having breakfast on her deck, she hit the gym. Thinking while on the elliptical trainer about what she would say to Sushma and anticipating every possible objection to her arguments about Kyle's bogus "information," she hammered away, breaking her personal record for calories burned in half an hour. *A good sign.*

Wearing the carbon gray Armani business suit Chartre had picked out for her, Lara felt pumped when she entered Sushma's ICE House office.

"I'd like to speak to Ms. V," Lara said to the assistant. She had never been told to call Sushma "Ms. V," but since everyone else in the organization did, Lara thought it would be good to act as though she thoroughly belonged.

"Oh, good," the assistant said. "Then, you got my text?"

"Text?"

"I know, I sent it kind of late. But since you're here, it's cool."

The assistant hit a button on her phone. "Miss Dixon is here."

"Send her in." Sushma managed to sound cold even through a speakerphone.

The grim décor spooked Lara. *The desk looks like a casket, the chairs like instruments of torture. And that painting looks like the aftermath of a nuclear bomb. No wonder she's always so grumpy.*

Sushma remained seated and focused on the desktop monitor. "Good morning, Miss Dixon."

Not a smidge of warmth. "Good morning."

"Have a seat. Would you like tea?"

"Thank you, but I'm not—"

"It is Tieguanyin," Sushma said, finally making eye contact with Lara.

Lara waited for more information as Sushma calmly poured herself a cup of a liquid that, when sunlight passed through it, took on a deep amber hue.

"I take it you do not know about Tieguanyin?"

Lara shook her head.

"Smell the leaves," Sushma said, pointing to the box. Lara leaned forward and saw that the box, which appeared to be quite old, held a ceramic bowl full of tea leaves, a wooden scoop and a bamboo whisk.

"Pick up the bowl and hold it close to your nose."

Lara carefully raised the scoop to her face and took a whiff. It had a strong, flowery aroma.

"Interesting," Lara said.

"I would say so." Sushma sipped her tea. "This is spring Tieguanyin, fully baked in accordance with very ancient and strictly guarded traditions. It is one of the rarest teas in the world, and it costs one thousand, five hundred dollars per pound."

"Oh!" Lara put the bowl down reverently.

"Do not tell me you are worried about what might happen if you dropped it."

"At fifteen hundred dollars a pound, I'd rather not find out."

Sushma picked up the bowl, took two steps to

the deck and committed the tea leaves to the wind. "Fast Lane," she said, "can afford to lose a few paltry measures of tea."

Nice display, but I won't be so easily intimidated today.

"Tieguanyin is named after a Buddhist deity." Sushma sipped from her cup. "The Iron Goddess of Mercy. Are you sure you do not wish to try some?"

"I'm sure. Look, the reason I came here—"

"The reason you came here is that I sent for you."

"I never got a message."

"I see. Then, please, by all means, tell me why it is that you came to my office."

Lara moved back in the chair and placidly smoothed out wrinkles in her skirt.

"It's about the...material...you showed me yesterday."

Sushma looked at her without expression.

"I assume you were trying to...warn me...about something that might be a cause for concern."

Still no hint of emotion.

"I thought you'd be interested in hearing my side of the story before you made any judgments."

Sushma took another sip of tea.

"My ex-husband is not what you'd call a... reliable...source of information. At least, not about me—and certainly not about our marriage. He tried to pull something like this during the divorce, but backed off because he was afraid of a little thing called perjury."

Lara wanted to say more, but the divorce had taught her to offer only as much information as was absolutely required.

"Is that all you have to say?" Sushma asked.

Lara nodded. Sushma put down the teacup and stood up.

"Once a woman is officially brought into the organization, she will never be left wanting again." She looked at the blank wall and paced, very slowly, behind her desk. "If she wishes to drink the best tea in the world, gallons of it will be provided. If she desires to own a thousand pair of shoes, they will be delivered to her door. If her dream is to produce movies or to create a charity that will feed a million people, she will have access to the best contacts and all the capital such undertakings require. I am talking about lifetime privileges. This is true for anyone who has sat in your position."

She stopped, turned on her heels and looked at Lara. Directly. Accusingly. "Members of The Rotation are royalty in the eyes of the company."

Now Lara sat expressionless. *Where is this heading?*

Sushma turned toward the window and resumed pacing. "What the company asks in return is that you meet certain standards. Do not use illegal drugs. Do not become involved in embarrassing public scenes. Refrain from excessive partying and carrying on. Do not do anything that would harm the functioning of the company."

She stopped. "Or its image."

Okay. I get it.

Sushma turned to Lara. "Your entrée to The Rotation was exceptional. In every other instance, candidates were thoroughly vetted before being invited to join us." She paused for a long time, keeping her eyes trained on Lara. "May I ask why you believe I would be concerned about the...material...as you call it?"

"You're worried people will think I won't be faithful to one man," Lara replied. "The whole idea of The Rotation works only if people believe all these women are devoted to Clay while he remains free 'n' easy and...and in charge."

Sushma nodded. "Again, you demonstrate that you are at least not stupid."

Lara ignored the left-handed compliment. "That's not what concerns *me*, though." She rose to her feet. "What concerns me is what that lying S.O.B. told you is simply not true."

"You are certain of it?"

"Of course."

Sushma opened the top drawer of her desk, took out a slim remote control, aimed it at the ceiling monitor and clicked.

Grainy video footage, obviously shot with a security camera in insufficient light, appeared on the screen. A naked woman, blond hair hanging down over her face, on all fours. A man entering her from behind. The woman sweeping her hair to one side. The man leaning over to fondle her breasts.

Lara's jaw dropped. *What the fuck?*

The man: Kyle's brother, Drake. The woman: Lara.

Sushma did not watch the monitor. She kept her eyes on Lara. "You are certain of it still?"

Lara felt woozy. She fought off panic. *No way I'm passing out in front of this bitch again.*

"This is wrong," Lara said, her throat tight.

"I am glad to hear you acknowledge it."

"That's not what I mean—and you know it."

"So, first you are telling me there is something that I do not know, and now there is something that I do?"

"This is fake. I don't know how...but it's fake. I would *never*—" She looked up at the screen and grimaced. Her stomach turned—from stress *and* from the very thought of having any part of Kyle's slimy brother inside her.

"I am not an expert in such matters," Sushma said as she clicked off the video. She opened the drawer again and pulled out a sheet of paper. "However, I have an affidavit signed by your ex-husband which attests that what you have just seen has not been altered or manipulated in any way. A *legal* document." She thrust it toward Lara. "Would you like to examine it?"

Lara gritted her teeth. "Whether I examine it or not, it's still a sham."

She walked to the door deliberately, working hard to retain her dignity. She was tempted to slam the door behind her, but her better judgment won out and she closed it gently, nodded to Sushma's assistant, and left.

SIXTEEN

*O*ut in the hall, Lara took a moment to collect herself. *Okay, this is bad. But how bad?* Lara's divorce had been messy, but she never expected Kyle would stoop so low as to fake a sex tape. Even if she proved it was fake, she would be seen as just another bimbo who'd gained fifteen minutes of fame by simply spreading her legs.

And lose Clay.

So, pretty bad.

As she headed back to her suite, a door behind her opened—the door to Corynne's suite. Lara glanced back as Corynne stepped out. *Just who I wanted to see.* Lara smiled politely, intending to dash off, but Corynne smiled at her, oddly triumphant. Lara's heart skipped a beat when someone else exited the suite.

Clay.

Some previous commitment!

Clay never saw Lara. Corynne swung him around, looked into his eyes and said, "It was a wonderful night, Clay. It always is when I'm with you."

She kissed him, but trained her knife eyes on Lara. Lara spun and bolted around the corner.

* * *

Lara raced through the labyrinthine halls of the ICE House, heedless of where she was going. She turned a corner and slammed into Taequanda.

"My, my, my. Someone's gotten herself all worked up into a situation."

You don't know the half of it. Out of breath, Lara kept her head down in a futile attempt to stop Taequanda from seeing her tears. "I'm sorry, I just—" The tears came even harder.

Taequanda put an arm around Lara. "Why don't we step into my room so we can talk about it?"

"No, I'll be all right. Really." Lara's face was streaked, her eyes puffy and red.

"I can see that." Taequanda sounded like a mom in a sitcom.

Lara half-laughed through the tears.

"You know," Taequanda said, "we don't *have* to talk. We'll just drink some tea and make chit-chat an option."

Tea? But Lara followed Taequanda into the suite.

242

It was a feast for the eyes. Original African paintings featuring stylized dancers in outlandish headdresses adorned red-orange walls accented with rich purple streaks. A potted aloe plant rose like a spiny bonfire in tongues of flame that were green at the base with dusty burgundy tips. Fierce three-foot-tall wooden war masks lorded over the room from one wall, while a mahogany dresser guarded by intricately woven raffia dolls stood sentinel against another. Between them sat a papasan chair mounded with Beanie Babies.

And then there were the paintings, photos and figurines of naked women in amorous poses with other women. *What's up with those?*

"Really nice," Lara said. "Interesting."

"It's the room I always imagined when I was a teenager. 'Course, I was a very messed-up teenager."

Taequanda put two mugs of water into a microwave oven. "Check this out." She opened a tea box and held it up to Lara's nose. The powder had strong mint overtones.

"Nice. What kind is it?"

"I don't know. I just tell my P.A. to get me more when the box is low."

"It's not Tieguanyin."

"The Iron Goddess of Mercy. The vaunted Ms. V thinks she's all about that tea, which she may be— except," Taequanda counted off the points on her fingers, "she's not so tough, not much of a goddess and wouldn't know mercy if it bit her in the ass. But she's right about one thing: She is as nasty as that shit tastes."

"She said it costs fifteen hundred dollars a pound."

"Like costing the most makes it the best."

"It smells good."

"It does. But what difference does that make if you don't like it?"

The microwave beeped. Taequanda motioned for Lara to sit in one of two rattan chairs near the window. Lara looked out as Taequanda mixed a spoonful of tea into each mug.

"Now, this," Taequanda said, handing Lara a steaming mug, "this is something God herself thought up."

Herself?

Lara gazed into the mug. Sparks of golden light reflected off the wavy surface. Sumptuous clouds of steam bathed her face. She could feel the red disappear from her eyes and the confusion from her mind.

"Go on, drink," Taequanda said. "I don't make it too hot."

"I was just wondering—what is it with tea around here?"

Taequanda sat in the other chair. "It's like everyone's a pusher, right? I used to hate tea. But, then, they don't have anything like this at the Albertson's."

Lara took a sip—and it was heavenly. Peppery *and* sweet.

"You know what messed me up when I was a kid?" Taequanda mused.

Lara shook her head.

"My parents."

"Your parents?" Lara couldn't help glancing around at all the female erotica.

"Oh, I see. I was going to say my parents because they were too normal. You were thinking maybe I had some kind of conflicted sexuality." Taequanda had an admonishing look, but a teasing tone.

"I didn't mean—"

Taequanda tapped Lara's knee. "Lots of people think that. But, believe you me, there was no conflict. I knew I wanted to be with girls all along. That's right. I am a lezz-bee-an. Lez-bo. One hundred percent, dyed-in-the-wool, DNA-fueled Daughter of Sappho. You're cool with that, right?"

"Of course," Lara said. *No blondes allowed at Fast Lane—but a lesbian's okay?* "Taequanda—"

"Tae-Q."

Lara smiled. It felt good to be included in the Between Girls Club. "Tae-Q, how did you come to be in The Rotation?"

"Usual way. I knew people who knew people who got me an interview."

An interview? That's the usual way?

"An interview with whom?"

Taequanda shrugged. "This one and that one—you know, peons—and then the Dragon Lady herself."

Lara's body tensed and her brain whirred and clicked, like a hard drive struggling to download a really big file.

"Unless," Taequanda said, "you mean it like, how did I come to be in The Rotation when I don't necessarily fit the profile?"

"It did cross my mind."

"I can see that, so you don't have to look so stressed." Lara relaxed. Taequanda put a hand on her knee. "There we go. 'Cause we're, like, between girls here, right?"

Lara nodded.

Taequanda leaned toward Lara. "It's nothing didn't cross my mind. When Ms. V-for-Viper told me, I wondered why. I knew the answer once I was inside: That man's in every bed from here to Timbuktu and back again—in everybody's head. But I swear I've scored more pussy in each of my eleven months than Double C's gotten the whole damn time."

Lara laughed. "You do have a way with words."

"My only way is to say what needs to be said. And what I need to say to you is that Clay Creighton's a changed man since you showed up."

"He is?"

"You don't know? He thinks you're the aurora borealis, Liberty's torch and—"

"The leprechaun's pot o' gold all rolled into one?"

"Leprechaun's pot o' gold? I guess that works. I was going to say the shekinah glory."

"The *what?*"

"Yeah. Most people don't know what that is."

Lara laughed. "*I* don't know what that is, but I'm guessing it's not a bad thing."

"No, it is not a bad thing. Not a bad thing at all."

They sat in silence, nodding.

Lara finished her tea. "Well." They both stood up.

"Whatever made you shoot down that hallway, tears spilling down your face like a waterfall," Taequanda said, "you've got to shine your light on that. Shine the light that comes from deep down inside, and you'll find the answer."

Lara hugged Taequanda. "I hope so."

"I didn't say 'hope so,'" Taequanda said. "I said what I did because, what's my way?"

"To say what needs to be said."

"That's right. Don't let anybody write your story for you. Say what needs to be said. Write your own story."

SEVENTEEN

Sushma stood on the deck and shook her head. "What is he doing down there?"

Morgan Hopkins stepped to the rail and looked down to find Clay crawling around on the rocks, poking his head into cracks and digging around with his hands.

"I certainly don't know, Ms. V," he answered. "Would you like me to go ask him and report back to you?"

"Fuck that," she said. "I will go find out myself."

* * *

A cool breeze blew off the water, but the sun had already burned away the fog and warmed the air. Sushma marched from the stairs that hugged the cliffside into the stark light.

Clay looked up. "Shush? Going to work on your tan?"

"Tan, my ass. What is the meaning of this?"

"I wouldn't mind if you tanned your—"

"Do not attempt to amuse me with your sopho-moric jokes. Why are you not preparing for the meeting with the lingerie people?"

Clay's focus returned to the recesses between boulders. "Usually, you have me at 'lingerie.' But I'm pretty tired right now."

"Which is exactly why you should not be doing whatever it is you are doing out here."

"You'll be at the meeting, right?"

"Of course."

"Then I'm as prepared as I need to be."

Sushma threw up her hands. "You are incorrigible."

"Don't worry. I'll toss it to you and sit there and act like I know what you're talking about. Just like always."

"When will you start giving your business the respect it deserves?"

"Maybe today wouldn't be the best time." Clay reached into a fissure and dug out a stone. "Who scheduled a morning meeting for me after an over-night air strike?"

"You could have slept on the helicopter."

Clay stood up and stepped to another rock. "I did sleep on the helicopter. I woke up more tired than before."

"I have spoken to Miss McFee, and she did not appear to be tired."

"Corynne's twenty-one, Shush. I could function on three hours of sleep at that age, too."

"Corynne is twenty-*three*."

"Whatever." Clay knelt and dropped his head into a crack between two boulders.

"Why *are* you out here?" Sushma demanded.

Clay answered, but his voice echoed around the crevice, so Sushma gingerly stepped onto the rock with him.

"Lara's phone," he said.

"How in the world did her phone get down here?" Sushma looked suspiciously at Lara's deck, sixty feet overhead.

"I spooked her. She dropped the phone."

Sushma's anger smoldered. "How did you 'spook' her?"

"Long story."

"Why would you waste time looking for a stupid phone? If Miss Dixon is in need of a new one, we will simply issue it to her. In fact, should she not already have been issued a corporate phone?"

"Maybe I'm just doing it to be nice." He poked his head farther into the cavern where water slapped against granite.

Sushma moved toward the steps, then stopped. She looked up at Lara's deck again, then down to Clay. Then she took out her own phone and hit a few buttons. Sushma followed the ringtone as fast as her pumps could carry her to where the phone was wedged into a crease where grass grew in pebbly sand.

Clay bounded to the site, too, but not before Sushma scraped aside gravel and pried the phone free.

"Good work," Clay said, holding out his hand. Sushma turned her back on him and flipped the phone open.

"Come on, Shush. Give the girl a little privacy."

Sushma turned around with that gunslinger look. Clay stepped back as though he'd been pushed.

"What?"

"Do you recognize this name?" Sushma pushed a key and held up the phone so Clay could see the screen.

"I really don't care wha—" His mouth dropped open, his shoulders went limp and his chest deflated as Sushma played Gina's message.

Sushma self-righteously snapped the phone shut and marched up the steps. Clay sat down and fidgeted with the fishbowl gravel as he stared into a dark hole between two rocks.

EIGHTEEN

*L*ara left Taequanda's suite with a clear mind. *Time to lay everything on the table with Clay.* Telling Clay how she felt about him might make everything right—or get her a limo ride back to Santa Monica. One thing was certain: If Clay had spent the night with Corynne, Lara had more reason than ever to want to destroy him. *But how do you destroy someone you love?*

Lara's resolve took a hit, though, when she turned into the corridor that led to her suite. Two guards stood sentry at the open door. Chartre's workers wheeled out a rack of clothing. Sushma barked orders from inside the room. Lara's heart pounded.

"Miss Dixon?"

Lara whirled to see Morgan Hopkins.

"I want to apologize for what's going on here, but we did try to locate you beforehand."

If I'm going to be tossed out, it's nice to know I'll be tossed out by a gentleman.

Lara glanced back toward her suite. "What *is* going on?"

"Ms. Vishnuveda is waiting to speak with you. I'm sure she'll be happy to explain everything."

I'm sure she'll be ecstatic.

Morgan guided Lara past the guards. The room went silent. Assistants and security personnel stepped aside to let Sushma approach Lara. "I will speak to you outside."

Sushma marched onto the deck. No one made eye contact with Lara as she looked around the room. She straightened her jacket and joined Sushma.

* * *

Sushma stood like an avenging angel. "You understand what is happening here?"

Lara nodded.

"Do you understand why?"

"My guess is it has something to do with the conversation we had earlier."

"That guess would be incorrect." Sushma flipped open Lara's phone and held it up so Lara could see Gina's name and number on the screen. "You know who this is, yes?"

Shit.

Lara nodded.

"Then it is obvious," Sushma said as she snapped the phone shut, "why you cannot continue to stay here."

Lara scanned the view. The ocean, so blue, and the sky, so clear, blended in a soft-focus haze.

"There will be a car to take you back to Santa Monica. Mr. Hopkins and his people will escort you out. Your belongings have already been loaded."

"I didn't bring any belongings with me."

"I am referring to items that you acquired during your stay. Clothing and other amenities."

"I don't want them."

"Nonetheless, they are yours. It is so stated in your contract. And Fast Lane," Sushma said, making a point of looking Lara directly in the eye, "honors its contracts."

The two women studied each other.

"Tell me—" Lara started.

"There is nothing more that I wish to say to you or hear from you at this time," Sushma interrupted. "Any further communication between you and any-one associated with this company will be achieved through attorneys. And by referring to *anyone*, I mean *everyone*."

Sushma brushed past Lara to the door.

"I'm not asking about business," Lara said.

Sushma waved her hand dismissively and reached for the door. Lara jammed the door with her foot.

"Tell me the truth," Lara said.

Sushma laughed. "You have quite a nerve demanding such a thing."

Lara looked Sushma square in the eye. "You love Clay."

Sushma's eyes flashed, a brief—but telling—break in her facade. The look on her face went from deadpan to just plain deadly.

"I will tell you nothing of the sort!" She barged her way inside.

* * *

Lara's heart felt cold and clenched, like snow being pressed into an ice ball. The door opened and Tiffany stumbled out.

Tiffany went white. "Oh, I didn't..." Her eyes dropped. "I didn't know anyone was out here." She turned to go back inside.

"Were you spying on me?" Lara's voice held no harshness.

"Yes," Tiffany said without turning around.

"Did you learn anything?"

"I did."

"What?"

Tiffany turned around, still looking at the floor. "I learned that...that you're..." She swallowed hard.

"That I'm what?"

Tiffany's eyes rose to meet Lara's. "In love with Mr. C."

The ice in Lara's heart began to melt.

"I mean, any idiot could see that," Tiffany continued, averting her eyes again.

"Is that all?"

Tiffany shifted her feet. In spite of her whimsical purple sneakers with orange- and-red-striped laces, she looked guilty as hell.

Things are never how they look at Fast Lane. Lara put a hand on Tiffany's shoulder. "You knew about my association with Gina Wray, too."

Tiffany nodded. "I saw your phone."

"But you didn't tell anyone, did you?"

Tiffany wiggled her shoulders.

"You could have gotten fired for not telling Sushma."

Water welled up in Tiffany's eyes as she peered at Lara through her bangs. "I mean, you were in love. Narking someone out for that just seemed, you know, wrong."

A half-smile formed on Lara's lips. "Your secret's safe with me. You know—between girls."

Tiffany fell sobbing into Lara's arms. "If it means anything," she sniffed, "I thought you were a decent boss. I mean, you know, in the extreme."

The door opened and Morgan bowed politely. "I'm sorry, Miss Dixon."

Lara acknowledged him with a look. "It does mean something, Tiffany," she said. "It means a lot."

They smiled at each other.

"Oh! Wait!" Lara dashed inside and returned with the slinky, shimmery, sequin-covered Donna Karan tank. "This is yours."

Tiffany's mouth dropped open. "Oh, Miss D...."

Lara hugged her again. "I'm not a personage anymore. You can call me Lara."

Still sobbing, Tiffany turned and smacked into Morgan. She bounced backward, clutched the shirt to her bosom and bolted.

"She going to be all right?" Morgan asked as the girl disappeared.

"She'll be even better than that. Okay if I look at the view one more time?"

Morgan nodded.

Lara had looked at a very similar view from the bluffs of Santa Monica dozens, maybe hundreds, of times in the last couple of years. But looking toward Santa Monica from across the bay, with Paradise Cove on one side and Point Dume on the other, made it clear just how close—and how far apart—the worlds that made up Los Angeles could be.

As Lara turned to go, something below caught her eye.

Clay.

"Yes," Lara said. "I'm ready."

* * *

No one spoke as Morgan and three guards escorted Lara onto an elevator to the ground floor. People sneaked glances at her as the somber procession passed their work spaces. Neither Morgan nor any of his assistants laid a hand on her.

Such gentlemen. Would I feel guilty if I just...

Lara suddenly broke ranks and slipped through a door to steps that led to the water.

And Clay.

He reacted not at all to her presence. He just kept sifting rocks.

Morgan and the other guards arrived at the bottom of the steps. Lara looked back at them plaintively, and Morgan led his cohort out of earshot.

"I want you to know something."

Still Clay did not look at her. "I already know too much." He sounded tired.

"I don't think you do."

Clay pulled up a handful of scraggly grass and let the blades flutter away in the breeze. "I heard the voice message."

"It's true. I came here on a mission. I was mad because I thought you gave my ex-husband the idea he could have a Rotation of his own. I made up this plan and sold Gina on the idea."

"She got Anton Roche to say all those nice things about you?"

"I don't know if it matters, but most of that stuff was true." She bit her lip. "The conversation we had that first night, what we talked about...I had to do a bunch of research to make it look like we had something in common. To fool you into thinking I was your kind of woman. But, you seemed to be really interested in me, and that made me more interested in that stuff." Her voice trailed off. "And in you."

She paused. *Give me some kind of reaction. Resignation. Anger. A shrug, even.* "I'm not a bad person. In fact, I thought I could do a lot of people some good if I—"

"Cut me down to size—and make a million dollars while you were at it?"

Lara hung her head. "I was wrong. About everything." She swallowed hard, fighting tears. Tears were winning. "I know that now. I knew it a week ago, but I didn't know what to do. I was in over my head. I kept trying to climb out."

"Well, you're out now," Clay said, "and you didn't have to do anything."

Lara stepped toward him. "Clay, I—"

"Stop," he said. Lara could hear the disappointment in his voice, and that hurt more than anger or meanness ever could. "I'm not in the mood for a big discussion."

"I thought—"

Clay shook his head. "I said I don't want to talk."

"Then don't," Lara said. "But I thought we had something. I thought that, in spite of everything—the deception—there was something real. I felt it—and I thought you felt the same. That first night, when we talked about love and war...I never had a conversation like that with a man. Or anyone, for that matter. Not since my dad..." She swallowed hard. "The salt flats. The waterfall at Heat. Didn't any of that mean anything to you?"

"Fun times." Sarcasm poisoned Clay's words.

"That's all?"

"I wanted you to feel like—"

"Like what? The center of the universe?"

Clay shrugged. "If that's what you want to believe."

"It's not what I *want* to believe. But if it's true, you can't hate me for lying and leading you along. You were deceiving me, too."

"*I* was deceiving *you*?"

"You made me believe we did have something special. Like I was the center of your universe. And then you slept with Corynne."

"I *what*?"

"I'll bet you didn't have to sweet-talk *her*. She's already the center of her own universe."

Clay stood up. "You're crossing a line—"

"*I'm* crossing a line?" Lara stepped onto the rock

with Clay and tapped his chest with her finger. "*You* left *my* side to go spend the night with *her*! Or are you going to tell me that was just business?"

"I guess it depends on how you define 'business.' We had an appearance in Seattle. For charity."

Lara's heart jumped.

"We didn't sleep together. In fact, I didn't get any sleep. I was too wound up thinking about you."

"That was your 'previous engagement'?"

Clay turned away. "What difference does it make?"

It would have made all the difference in the world—an hour ago.

"Making appearances is part of my job, Lara. And Corynne's. It's what the girls in The Rotation do."

"But—"

"You have to leave now," Clay interrupted. "I'm meeting with the lingerie people in a few minutes. I believe you've met some of them." He took out his phone, pressed a button and spoke. "Do your job, Morgan."

Morgan came back down the steps and held out a hand to help Lara negotiate the rocks.

"Oh," Clay said, "the next time you see Virginia, tell her I understand."

Lara paused. "Who?"

"Ma'am, please," Morgan said.

Clay had turned back toward the water. Lara accepted Morgan's hand and headed up the stairs.

NINETEEN

*I*n Gina Wray's office the next day, Lara looked tired and beaten.

"Don't worry about that nondisclosure bullshit," Gina said. "Fast Lane has deep pockets, but we've got big guns on our side, too."

"It's not that I'm afraid to write about anything," Lara said. "It's that I don't have anything to write about."

"Oh, come on. You have *something*. You were there, on the inside. Hell, you had Clay Creighton *inside* you!"

Is that supposed to be a joke? "There isn't anything," Lara said.

Gina's face grew stern. "Didn't you come in here talking about how he's a monster and a prick and how he needs to be taken down—"

"I was wrong."

"—and how you had this great plan—"

Lara slouched. "I was wrong about that, too."

Gina sat down and kneaded her temples. "Let's think about this. What about the fact that he's not in charge? His loyal readers will love *that*, right? It's Fast Lane's thing: The man's in charge. And here is The Man, himself—*the* man among men—and his whole fucking life is run by a *woman*?"

"Hugh Hefner's daughter has run *Playboy* for years."

"Yeah, but he's old enough to be a grandfather. Hell, he's old enough to be *everyone's* grandfather. And, besides, no matter who's in charge, he still gets to pick his own blondes."

And Clay has Ms. V-as-in-Viper do it for—wait.

Lara's head came up off her hand. "You *know* that a woman calls the shots at Fast Lane?"

Gina's shoulders and neck stiffened. "Of course."

Lara sat up straight. "And you *know* Clay doesn't pick the women in The Rotation?"

Gina rummaged through papers on her desk. "For God's sake, *everyone* knows *that*."

"Actually, as far as I can tell, *almost nobody* knows that." Lara sat on the edge of the chair. "And they work very hard to keep it that way."

Gina got up and dug through the pockets of a jacket on a coat tree and pulled out her chrome-plated lighter. "That's something you can put in there, too, right? The great lengths they go to to keep people in the dark?"

Lara noticed Gina's hands shaking as she lit a cigarette. And that her chin was pointy. Lara mentally leafed through the photos of every woman who'd ever been in The Rotation. *So many with dark hair.* She looked down at her own painted chocolaty locks. *Every woman in The Rotation for the past six years had brown hair. Except for that red-headed slut, Corynne.*

Lara looked back up at Gina, still framed by the window. Smoke swirling around her caught the sunlight, making it look like she had a tangle of curls hanging over her face.

Lemony curls.

Lara jumped to her feet. "How much do you know about Fast Lane?"

"No more than anyone else. Stuff that's, you know, just out there. Media reports. Online sources. Rumors. For God's sake, there's rumors up the wazoo. Anyway, I'm sure we can block out your piece without too much trouble."

Gina paced behind her desk as she rambled on about the inner workings of Fast Lane's corporate structure, but Lara's eyes locked on the lighter, which Gina had tossed onto the desk. Specifically the engraved initials.

V.W.

"So you're a big fan of German cars?" Lara asked.

"What do German cars have to do with..." Gina followed Lara's gaze back to the lighter. Lara reached for it, but Gina dived over the desk and scooped it up.

"V.W.? Huh." Gina stared at the lighter as though she had never seen it before. "I never thought about it. I don't think it has anything to do with cars. It's just a cool piece I picked up at a vintage shop a few years back."

"I don't think it has anything to do with cars, either—Virginia."

"What are you—"

"Virginia *Warren*, to be specific. The woman who was in The Rotation for just a few weeks."

Gina's eyes narrowed to knife-edge slits. She tucked her hair behind her ears. Smoke escaped from her flared nostrils and pursed lips. She looked like a dragon preparing to blast a pesky villager. "What are you getting at?"

"I think we both know what I'm getting at. My question is, why get *me* involved?"

"Okay, let's just say I *am* this Virginia Warner." Gina took a deep pull on her cigarette. "So what?"

"It's *Warren*," Lara said, holding her steely gaze. "And this meeting is over."

Gina stormed across the room and cut Lara off at the door. "I don't think so."

"Well, then, feel free to go on without me." Lara

reached across Gina and opened the door. "Oh, and I have a message for you: Clay says he understands."

"Oh, does he?" She coughed. "You go tell Clay-boy to fuck himself! Because one thing's for sure, he's never going to be fucking *you* again. He has plenty of better options."

Lara looked deep into Gina's eyes and saw rage boiling in her soul the way smoke billowed from her throat. And something more.

Pain.

Lara felt her own rage subside. "Now I understand."

"What do you understand?"

"You loved him."

Gina half-spat, half-laughed a mouthful of smoke into Lara's face. "*Every* woman loves Clay Creighton."

Lara was unfazed. "But he loved you back, so you had to go."

"What a fucking joke!"

"You *still* love him."

"I'll tell you what you understand." Gina's voice rose by one octave and several decibels. "You understand jack shit. But my lawyers will be happy to enlighten you."

"How did they do it? Fake sex tape? Or did they slip something into your tea that made you fail a drug test?"

"I don't have to listen to this anymore." Gina stabbed Lara's chest with the fingers that held her cigarette, flicking ash onto Lara's top. "You signed a contract, and when you get hit with a million-dollar judgment for not living up to it, you'll understand something, that's for goddamn sure."

Lara moved Gina's hand away and brushed off the ashes. "Don't worry. I have every intention of keeping our agreement." She exited calmly, closing the door behind her.

Gina threw open the door and yelled after Lara, "I don't care what you write—you and Clay Creighton can both go fuck yourselves!"

She slammed the door, then jerked it right back open. "And the same goes for that whore, Sushma Vishniedoodoo!"

TWENTY

*L*ara spent the next couple of days in seclusion, writing Gina's article. She left her apartment only to let in the Salvation Army guys who were there to pick up the clothes from Fast Lane. *Someone might be thrilled to buy a $1,400 hand-painted Dolce & Gabbana T-shirt for $6.95.* She threw in the clothes she had gotten from Gina, too. Including the crimson dress she never got to wear.

While in the lobby, she also picked up her mail. Her new phone had come, but she was in no hurry to even take it out of the box. She didn't care if anyone tried to call her and didn't plan to answer if they did.

The first draft poured out of her, but she revised carefully, double-checking sources and weeding out innuendo. She emailed her final draft to Gina first, and then to Sushma.

Gina's reply came just a few hours later "My lawyers will be contacting you—and don't think you can avoid them by not answering your phone."

The next day Lara received a terse reply from Sushma: "Where and when would you like to meet?" Lara suggested lunch at a market in the valley on Sunday. She needed to visit the area anyway, so why not consolidate trips?

* * *

Sunday's excursion began with Lara pulling into the driveway of an unassuming Chatsworth bungalow and parked next to an SUV so big and shiny it made her Taurus look like a rusty tin can. Lara cut through scraggly desert plants and weeds toward a chain-link fence laced with green plastic privacy strips. Shimmying through an opening between the house and the fence, she heard exactly what she expected to hear: bubbling water and bimbos in a hot tub.

A bleached-blonde with enough silicone in her chest to fill a three-layer Jell-O mold saw Lara first. A redhead was preoccupied, what with her mouth being full of Kyle's cock.

"Oh-oh," the blonde said. "I think the meter maid's here."

"Meter reader?" Sitting on the edge of the Jacuzzi, Kyle couldn't be bothered to open his eyes until the blonde poked him. When he saw Lara, he hollered, "Oh, shit," then shoved the redhead into the froth between his legs.

"Lara—what the fuck?"

Apparently the Mae Wests affixed to the redhead's torso made her too buoyant to stay under for long. She came up spitting water from her collagen-engorged lips. "I was thinking the exact goddamn thing," she sputtered.

"Then we're all on the same page," Lara said, "because that's *exactly* what I was thinking."

"Lara...sweetie...you're going to have to be a little more specific."

"The footage you gave to Sushma Vishnuveda."

"Who?"

"Is that the Japanese chick? Are we going to do some kind of interracial girl-on-girl thing?" the blonde asked.

The redhead nodded in Lara's direction. "That's cool. But who's *this* bimbo?"

Lara ignored them.

"Chill, ladies, I'll take care of this. Lara and I have history." Kyle's smile was so snaky Lara swore she could see a forked tongue flitting through his teeth. "Lara, really. I—" He stopped. "You know, you look really good."

"Oh, for—"

"No, really. Something's different. Did you..." He

raised his eyebrows and cupped his hands on his chest.

"That's right, Kyle," Lara said, "I got a boob job. They're all over the place now."

"I knew it," Kyle said.

"*She* got a boob job?" the blonde sneered.

"Yeah, what was she before? An A-cup?" the red-head chimed in.

"Double A," the blonde said. "She looks like an A now."

The redhead nodded.

Lara glared at all three of them in turn, then went into the house.

"What's up *her* ass?" the blonde asked.

"It's probably fake, too," the redhead said.

Lara came back with a toaster and an extension cord.

"Jesus!" the redhead said. "What's she gonna—"

"Just relax," Kyle said. "She's not going to do anything. Isn't that right, Lara?"

Lara calmly plugged the toaster into the extension cord and the extension cord into an outlet, then stepped up to the edge of the tub.

"Christ and candy bars! She's a psycho!" The redhead knocked Kyle into the water and used his submerged body to clamber onto the deck. The blonde didn't need a boost; the sudden tensing of every muscle in her body shot her out of the pool like a rocket.

Kyle stood up, but before he got any closer to

safety, Lara shook the toaster and said, "One more step and you're toast."

Kyle eased himself back to a sitting position, keeping both hands on the edge of the tub. "Toast," he said with a fake chuckle. "I get it. Good one."

"I'm done joking around. Let's talk about Sushma Vishnuveda. From Fast Lane?"

"Fast Lane." Recognition spread over Kyle's face. "I don't remember anyone name Vooshma, though. There was a guy."

"There was a *guy*?" the redhead interjected. "You got some kind of male-on-male thing going on?"

"Please, babe, I'll explain everything," Kyle said to her. "It's just that, you see, I'm in kind of a spot right now." He turned back to Lara. "A private investigator. Looked like a gangster from an old movie. He was digging around for dirt."

"Lucky for him he came here. Where else could he get a video of your vomit-inducing brother fucking me doggy-style?"

"You fucked my brother?"

"You fucked his *brother*?" the blonde said, crinkling her nose.

"*Doggy-style*?" the redhead said, making the same face as the blonde.

"She *is* a whore," the blonde concluded.

The redhead nodded. "I've never fucked someone's *brother*."

"What about the football twins from UCLA?"

"It doesn't count when both brothers are *right there*."

"Good point."

Lara slapped the toaster. "Sushma?"

"Okay, okay. Let me get out of the tub so we can go inside and talk this over."

"I kind of like you as toast." Lara looked at the bimbos. "How 'bout it, ladies?"

"Lara?"

She grinned and let go of the toaster.

* * *

Kyle frantically looked through files on his computer with Lara looking over his shoulder. "It would have been nice to let me at least throw a towel around myself."

"You should be grateful I didn't let the toaster hit the water."

"Yeah, well, it came fucking close. What if you misjudged how long the cord was?"

"You'd be dead. Which wouldn't be so bad."

"Here it is." Kyle clicked on a file of Lara and him having sex.

"This isn't what I saw," Lara said.

Kyle clicked on another file. The woman with him in this scene wasn't Lara. The same was true of the next file he opened. And the next.

"*All* these are from four years ago?"

"They're arranged chronologically."

"Jesus—how many women did you fuck when you were married to me?"

Kyle shrugged. "How many women are there?"

"Keep clicking," Lara said through clenched teeth. Finally, the scene she had viewed in Sushma's office came up. "This is what I saw...except it was Drake instead of you." She shuddered.

"I'm sorry about that," Kyle said. "I mean...Drake."

"Did you give the private eye any other footage? Something with Drake in it?"

"No. Just this."

"Then how did his face get plastered onto your body?"

"I don't know. Real estate guy. His face is everywhere."

Kyle clicked the mouse a few times to burn a DVD for Lara. She leaned on his desk and drummed her fingers. *Oh, for Christ's sake!* "Are you peeking down my dress?" Lara stood up. "You're such an asshole!"

"What? I've seen them before."

"You don't get to anymore."

"It's just that, from this angle, it doesn't look like, you know." Kyle cupped his hands at his chest again.

"I look different to you?" Lara asked in an irritated voice.

"Yeah. I gather it's not your boobs."

"Look at my *hair*, Kyle."

"You've got more of this showing?" He flicked his fingers on his own forehead. "It looks nice that way."

Seven fucking years of "cover your forehead, Lara."

"It's brown," she said

"It used to be a different color?"

Luckily for Kyle, the DVD tray popped open with Lara's copy of his home movies.

"You are just unbelievable," Lara said. "You have no trouble noticing the most miniscule details about any piece of ass that comes within a hundred feet of you—but after being married to me for seven years, you can't even say what color my hair was."

"Lighter brown! Right? With reddish streaks."

"Pathetic," Lara said. "You may continue your orgy now." She snatched the DVD and stormed into the backyard. The bimbos were still naked, reclining on lounge chairs and smoking cigarettes while waiting dutifully for Kyle.

"Bye, ladies," she said. "Enjoy the rest of your afternoon."

"Whore," the redhead said.

Lara stopped. "You realize, don't you," she said, "that he's filming everything you do in that hot tub."

"No fucking way!" the blonde responded.

Lara went up to a hanging planter, ripped out a microcam and tossed it in the bimbos' direction.

"No fucking way!" the redhead said.

"My guess is that if you look hard enough, you'll find two or three more stashed around the yard. He likes to catch every possible angle."

Lara squeezed back through the space between the fence and the house. Her car looked just as pathetic as before, but this time the noises she heard from the backyard made her smile.

TWENTY-ONE

*A*n hour later, Lara sat at a table under a sun-bleached umbrella in the midst of the bustling Encino Farmers Market. She laid out a paper napkin and arranged her lunch: a fish taco, a baseball-size cluster of champagne grapes and a slushy flavored with passion fruit and guava.

Sushma came to the table with a cup of fruit topped with a clear plastic dome. "I cannot believe you would pick such a place for our meeting."

"See anyone you know here?"

"In this godforsaken place? Do not be obscene."

Lara took a long pull of slushy through her straw and looked all around. Families. Teenagers. Senior citizens. *Not exactly Malibu or Rodeo Drive, but a pretty nice place for lunch on a Sunday.*

"This is really good," Lara said between slurps of her slushy. "You should try one."

"I would not put such a thing into my mouth."

"Why not? It's mostly fruit and ice."

Sushma didn't respond. She had managed to remove the plastic dome from the fruit cup and jabbed at chunks of pineapple, mango, grapefruit and apple before pushing the cup aside.

"Not hungry?" Lara asked.

"I am not in the mood for being in this place. Or for whatever game it is you are playing."

"*I'm* playing games?"

"If you are not, then explain to me why you showed me what you wrote for Virginia Warren."

"I wanted you to see that I can tell the truth."

"Your article is accurate. But one can be accurate and still not tell the truth."

Lara washed down the last bit of taco with a gulp of slushy. "So, we're on the same page. At least about that."

"This is exactly what I am not in the mood for. You apparently believe you know a great deal more than you are letting on, so why not simply say so?"

Lara put her new phone on the table so Sushma could see Kyle's footage playing on the screen. "Recognize this?"

"Of course I do."

"Look closer."

Sushma remained expressionless. "What is the point of this?"

"Is there a point to be made?"

Sushma stood up. "If you are insinuating that I or that anyone at Fast Lane altered this footage—"

"I'm not insinuating anything."

"This is absurd! Tell it to the attorneys."

"Tell them what? That you had this footage altered for the same reason you do everything else at Fast Lane?"

Sushma strode off. Lara grabbed the phone and followed. "You altered the footage for the same reason that you brought Taequanda into The Rotation."

"I brought Taequanda into The Rotation because she is beautiful and intelligent."

"And completely uninterested in Clay romantically."

Sushma walked faster. Lara kept pace.

"And you brought Corynne into The Rotation because you knew that Clay would have no interest in her, either."

"Do not be ridiculous. Why would any man not be interested in a woman such as Corynne?"

"Any man, sure—but not Clay."

"And why not?"

"Because she's twenty-three, shallow and self-absorbed—exactly the kind of woman Clay is no longer interested in. He's almost forty years old!"

"What difference does it make what age he is? Many men prefer younger women."

"Even so, don't you think he's old enough to pick out a woman for himself?"

Sushma waved dismissively. "You are making no sense."

"Does it make sense that no member of The Rotation since Gina—not one—has been blond?"

"Blondes represent a small minority of the world's population."

"Or even had light-brown hair?"

Lara got waylaid when Sushma darted between an older couple. *This is what Clay meant about love and war—and you can't stop me from taking my shots.* "And why did every woman since Gina have a boob job?"

The woman, who was generously endowed, gave Lara a dirty look.

"Those are real," the man said.

"I didn't mean her. Sorry." Lara slipped in between them and caught up to Sushma.

"This is Los Angeles," Sushma said. "*Every* woman has had a boob job."

"Not Gina."

"Stop following me, or I shall inform a police officer that I am being hounded by a disgruntled ex-employee."

"*You* said The Rotation is a business proposition. *You* said Clay isn't very good at business. *You* said the women who join The Rotation are usually thoroughly vetted."

Sushma walked even faster despite her four-inch heels.

"*You* are the one who does the vetting," Lara continued. "*You* decide who gets to be in The Rotation."

"Someone has to do it. Otherwise, there would be no quality control. Any gold digger or tramp or...or..."

"Or woman Clay might get attached to?"

Sushma stopped in her tracks. "Of course. If he should become attached, as you say, The Rotation would be threatened. And The Rotation is Fast Lane's bread and butter. I choose women according to what is best for the company."

"You don't do what's best for the company. You do what's best *for you*." Lara pointed at Sushma, stopping just short of touching her. "Gina—Virginia Warren—is everything you're not: Tall, blond—"

"And flat-chested?" Sushma spat out a laugh. "You are sounding more and more like a crazy person."

Sushma tried to brush past Lara and cross the street, but Lara grabbed her by the arm and pulled her back around.

"What do you think you are doing?" Sushma said, horrified.

"You love Clay," Lara said.

"Let go of me!"

"I only got into The Rotation so you could keep tabs on me while you figured out how to make me go away forever."

"I said let go!"

"You did the same thing with Gina!"

"I am warning you that I will scream!"

"Clay fell in love with Gina, flat chest and all, and

you decided she had to go. What did you do—fake some dirty pictures of her? Or did you have some other trick up your sleeve?"

"You must be a crazy person. How else could you have come up with such insane assertions?"

"It was in the media after you kicked her out: Clay brought her back to the ICE House after Elton John's Oscar party."

"Clay meets hundreds of women at those parties."

"But with Gina he skipped a step, didn't he? He skipped the step where you get to grill the girl to make sure there's no chance Clay will fall for her."

Sushma tugged harder to break free. "You do not know what you are talking about."

"The evidence is there. Every woman since Gina. A religious freak. An ultra-right-winger. A lesbian."

"I SAID—"

"You didn't find Gina. Clay did. And when it looked like they were getting too cozy, you stepped in with your 'dutiful C.O.O.' thing. And when Clay found me—"

Sushma yanked so hard, she broke Lara's grip and tumbled to the pavement. Lara stood over her with her fists and jaw clenched, air heaving in and out of her lungs. *Get up so I can knock you down myself, bitch.*

But Sushma did not get up. She remained seated on the hard concrete. Sobbing.

"All right! All right!" Sushma sat awkwardly with one leg underneath her. Her knees were scuffed and tears streamed down her face. "Everything you are saying is true! What of it?"

"I'll tell you what of it," Lara said, pointing an accusing finger in Sushma's face. "You had no right. You had no right to interfere in Clay's love life that way. No one has that right. Not even a chief operating officer."

"But I wanted *him.*"

"Well, you couldn't have him. And it wasn't just because of your hair color or your height or even your stupid fake boobs. For whatever reasons, he loved Gina. And he loved me. Don't ask me why. I don't meet the Fast Lane ideal. I'm an unemployed divorced woman who grew up a nobody in the valley. And every minute he's known me I've done nothing but lie to him. But for some reason, some reason we'll probably never know, he loved me. And you had no right to wreck that."

"He would have found out the truth about you eventually."

"Yes, but then we could have dealt with it. Him and me. Two people work things out. Or they don't. That's how it's supposed to happen."

Lara straightened and took a deep breath. "You may have stopped Gina and me from having Clay, but you'll never have him, either. Whatever he wants, you don't have."

Lara turned to walk away. She stopped when

Sushma sobbed, "Am I not beautiful? Am I not desirable? You came with your common valley upbringing and your failed marriage and your joke of a career—and your long legs and blond hair."

Lara touched her hair.

"That is right," Sushma continued. "Did you think I would not find out about that?"

"Magda wouldn't—"

"I did not learn it from Magda. It is my business to know such things. You may think I am stupid, but I saved Clayton from becoming a laughingstock. I made his company great and increased his wealth a hundred-fold. Am I not deserving of his love? More so than you?"

"He should love you because you made him rich?"

"There is more to it than that. I was, after all, a member of The Rotation."

"You're proud of that."

"Why would I not be? Only the most alluring, most cultured, most exciting women in the world get to be a part of The Rotation. Intelligent women who are charming and sexy and strong. For six years I have tried so hard to make him see me over all of the others. What is it? What is it that you have that I do not possess? Long legs and yellow hair?"

Unrequited love. I know how that feels.

Lara sat on the concrete next to Sushma. "I don't know if *it* is anything anyone can possess," she said. "*It* just...seems to happen."

286

Her lips still quivering, Sushma looked up. "You could tell how I felt about him from how I looked the other day. My eyes betrayed me."

"I could tell before that. Way before that."

"I thought some day he would grow up and see." Sushma sighed. "He is such a contradiction. The ultimate man of the world, and yet such a child."

"They're all a little like that, you know."

"Yes, I do know it. But, still, I kept hoping." Sushma rubbed one of her scraped knees. "I wanted to be his lover, but he saw me more like a mother. Sushma Vishnuveda, the stern Ms. V. The mother hen, clucking around, trying to work her stupid lovesick schemes. It is truly pathetic."

A shadow fell across Lara's face. She looked up to see a circle of onlookers. *Oh, my god! How much have these people heard?*

"Um, like, is everything cool?" asked a girl who reminded Lara of herself as a teenager.

"We'll be okay, but thanks," Lara said to the girl. Then, to everyone, she said, "Really. We'll be all right."

The crowd dispersed. Lara helped Sushma to her feet.

"Are you going to be okay?"

"I have been such a fool. I feel so worthless."

"You shouldn't think that way. You single-handedly saved Fast Lane. Everybody in the organization respects you."

"They do?"

"Sure."

"Even those who refer to me as Ms. V-for-Viper?"

You know about that? "I suppose. Deep down."

"Even you?"

"Of course!"

She looked away. "I have treated you very badly."

"Yes, you have. I kind of deserved it."

"Yes, you did." She looked at Lara. "However, I am sorry for one thing."

"Oh?"

"That business about Drake Lobo. I read about him on the Internet. He seems to be quite an asshole. I feel I should make it up to you in some way."

Lara studied Sushma's face. *Show me you mean it.* "Will you do something for me?"

Sushma swallowed hard. "I said I would, and I keep my word."

"Tell Clay I'll be hanging with Sol this evening."

"What does it mean, 'Hanging with Sol?'"

"He'll know what I mean."

Sushma nodded. "I will tell him."

"You're okay otherwise?"

"So-so. But a nice, strong cup of tea will work wonders."

Lara smiled. They nodded to each other, then walked off in opposite directions.

TWENTY-TWO

*C*lay slumped in a chair on the Upper Deck. The sun hung in the haze over the water, but Clay wasn't looking at the sun or the water. He wasn't looking at anything.

Sushma came onto the deck and leaned against the railing facing the water.

"What's up, Shush?"

Sushma didn't say or do anything. *This can't be good.*

"Shush?"

Sushma sat in a chair next to Clay, putting them eye to eye. Clay shifted in his seat. *This really can't be good.*

"Clayton," Sushma said in a softer voice than Clay was used to. "I wanted to ask you something."

Clay waited expectantly for several seconds. "Yes?"

Looking directly into his amber irises, she said, "What do you see in Lara Dixon?"

He jumped to his feet. "You mean what *did* I see?"

Sushma remained seated. *She looks so small from up here. Are those tears?*

"I want you to tell it to me straight," Sushma said. "No bullshit."

"Okay. She's pretty—but there was more to it than that. We had a few similar experiences growing up, which is weird when you think about our backgrounds. We had some nice conversations. She seemed to get me. I felt comfortable with her." His face darkened and his hands balled into fists. "Which was pretty goddamned stupid. I fell for her act, all right. Played right into her Big Plan."

"I do not believe that is true."

"What do you mean?"

"All of the women who have passed through The Rotation—especially during the past few years—were they all so unacceptable to you?"

"They were nice girls. Fun."

"Were you dissatisfied with their looks?"

"With their looks? No."

"Do you prefer women who are tall and fair and, shall we say, slender?"

"I don't have any problem with women who are short and dark and—" He stopped. *Wait a minute.* "What are you getting at?"

"You are saying that all of the women were beautiful, but you were looking for something more that was always missing?"

Clayed mulled it over. "Yeah. I guess."

"That did not happen by chance."

Clay crouched in front of her and took her hands in his. "What's going on?"

"Be truthful with me," Sushma said, trying to speak as though tears were not already rolling down her cheeks. "What is the number one thing you see in Lara Dixon?"

"The truth? I don't see anything in her. Not anymore."

"Are you certain?"

"She lied, Shush. She lied because she wanted to destroy me."

"Yes, that is true. However, sometimes a person's motives are pure, even though his or her actions may seem not to be."

For a man who's supposed to know so much about women, why can't I figure them out? "Okay. I'm completely lost."

Sushma looked down and spoke as quietly as Clay had ever heard her speak. "She is not the only one who has been lying to you."

Clay froze.

Sushma looked him in the eye. "I have done things that I am not proud of. Things that were not fair to you. I took control over parts of your life that I had no right to control. I said it was for the good of the business, but the real reason…"

She looked away and swallowed a sob.

Clay felt a wave of panic. *The "real reason."* *How obvious.* His mind raced, trying to identify signs he had missed—and he realized they had been everywhere.

"Oh, Shush. I feel like such an ass. Like a complete ass." He let go of her hands and stood up. He didn't know what else to say. As fond as Clay was of Sushma, he did not love her. And yet, though her eyes were red and cheeks streaked, she was as exotically beautiful as when she had joined The Rotation all those years before."But don't worry, I'll never have anything to do with Lara Dixon again. Ever."

"Whatever. Only you can decide whether to be an ass, or a complete ass." She started to leave, stopping halfway to the door. "There is one more thing. I promised to deliver a message from her. She said she would be hanging with Sol tonight. I do not know what that means. She said you would."

I would?

After Sushma left, Clay stood against the railing and looked out at the sun and the water and the haze in between.

TWENTY-THREE

*L*ara stood on her fingernail of a porch and remembered the phone ringing one Saturday morning. Could it really have been just a few weeks ago? Lara edged over to the corner and craned her neck to catch a glimpse of sky. She sighed. Why was it such a chore to catch even a glimpse of the beauty that existed all around her?

A half-hour till sundown.

Lara went back inside and contemplated a piece of clothing draped across the foot of the bed. A white cotton shirt. She smoothed it out, picked it up and held it to her face before slipping it on. Her eyes were immediately drawn to the plum-colored stain over her heart.

The shirt's tail moved with a breeze that wafted through the room. *Time to go.* She picked up her car keys and headed out.

* * *

A zephyr wind caressed Lara's hair as she approached the bluff at Ocean and Arizona. Point Dume looked like a glowing pot of gold at the end of an invisible rainbow. *I was there—but where was the gold?*

Lara brushed her hand across the stain on the shirt as she leaned against a railing and watched the sun make its inexorable descent. A noise came from behind her; she whipped around to find an old man and woman walking arm-in-arm.

"Eh, she look bootiful tonight, no?" The man grinned. The woman had bony shoulders and a wide bottom. Her gray hair was pulled back tight and she wore orthopedic shoes. The man was bent at the waist and limped. He had on brown Dacron pants, no doubt purchased during the Jimmy Carter presidency, and a silver-and-orange patterned shirt that never should have been sold to anyone anywhere. And it was buttoned wrong. But he smiled as wide as a man could smile.

They sure look happy together.

"Bootiful, yes?" the old man asked again. He nodded, but Lara couldn't tell if it was toward the sunset or the woman on his arm. They continued to a bench on the other side of a palm tree.

As the sun dipped behind the outcropping of rock so many miles away, the sky, the land and the water all burst into flames. It was the same every day, but Lara never got tired of seeing it. She closed her eyes, lifted her chin and took a deep, invigorating breath of cool, salty air.

And then another voice came from behind her.

"The view is amazing from here."

Lara's heart jumped. Though she gripped the railing, she could not feel her hands. Or her feet. Or anything else. Just a warm, buzzing electricity running through her body and soul. Lara wanted to open her eyes and run to Clay and embrace him and maybe even make love with him right there at the edge of the cliff, with the old couple just a few feet away and all the rush-hour traffic crawling by on the street.

"Yes, I've always loved the ocean."

"So have I. But I'm not talking about the ocean."

Lara turned around, and then slowly opened her eyes to see Clay just a few steps away. He had no Centurion cocktail in his hand. No beautiful escorts hanging on his elbows. Just Clay, his hands thrust into his pockets. His face was turned downward, but when he looked up at Lara, she could see the sunset, a dazzling array of purples and magentas and oranges, reflected in the golden rings of amber in his eyes.

"Oh, Clay..."

He moved close to her.

"Clay, I don't know where to begin."

"How about like this?" he said, putting his hands

on her waist and pulling her to him. The sunset glowed all around them in a kiss that lasted long enough to make up for the ones they had missed.

"I was so wrong about everything," Lara said when the kiss ended at last. "I wanted to destroy you, so I did terrible things and told terrible lies. I mean—look at this." She leaned forward and pulled on the part in her hair to show him the blond roots. "Even my hair."

The wind blew her hair off her forehead.

"I don't care what color your hair is," Clay said, "as long as it doesn't stop me from seeing your beautiful face." Then he put a hand under her chin and looked into her eyes. "I forgive you for whatever," he said, "as long as you forgive me."

"Forgive *you*?"

"The man you wanted to destroy deserved to be destroyed."

"I made a mess of things," Lara said.

"Yes, you did. I need to thank you for that."

"But, my idiotic plan."

"Idiotic? It *worked*."

Lara pulled back and waited for him to continue.

"You wanted to be the woman who ended The Rotation, right?"

Lara cringed.

"This is how the end of The Rotation comes to be: Clay Creighton falls in love."

Now Lara looked up into his eyes. He had the old

confidence. But not the swagger. Just sincerity. And tenderness. And humility.

"You're right," he said. "I haven't been telling you the truth, either. But I'll tell you the truest thing I ever knew: I love you, Lara Dixon. I've loved you since that first evening, when we talked all night about cars and sports and—"

"And whether love really is a battlefield?"

Clay outlined the wine stain with a finger. "And whether love really is a battlefield."

"Oh, Clay...I love you. I knew it then, too. I knew it—and I should have put an end to my stupid plan right on the spot."

"It wouldn't have done any good," he said. "We weren't ready."

"And we are now?"

He kissed her again, and suddenly the world was warm and cool and open and mysterious and bright and muddled—gloriously muddled—all at the same time. And she could live with it that way.

THE END

The opening to

Malibu
BRIDE
FAST LANE ROMANCE #2

DC THOME

AVAILABLE EARLY 2013

*T*he Malibu sunset was stunning. Tongues of reflected fire danced red and gold on Santa Monica Bay. Even the air glowed. But standing on the deck outside her office at Fast Lane Enterprises, Sushma Vishnuveda stared at her phone. It was time to make the call.

Why did I not see this coming?

For six years Sushma had worked day and night to save Fast Lane, the men's entertainment empire owned by notorious billionaire playboy Clay Creighton. The man Sushma loved. She had been so sure that someday he would love her back. And then Lara came along, intending to destroy him. But it was

Lara he fell for, destroying Sushma's hope of having him as her own.

It is my own fault. I wanted him as a lover, but he saw me as a colleague. Mixing business and romance? Never again.

Sushma felt her certainty grow. She had to change the way she related to men. The way she spoke. The way she carried herself. She turned her back on the sunset and faced her office window. It reflected a petite woman with eye-catching curves and full, sexy hair. But Sushma saw a body that needed to be taller and straighter and hair that was too thick. In short, she saw everything that Lara Dixon was not.

The way I look—that will have to change, too.

And the first step toward creating the New Sushma was to make the call.

Sushma flipped through the contacts on her phone until she came to Holt Richards. Or, more precisely, HRP. Holt's company was one of Hollywood's premiere packaging agencies, working out deals that brought top talent—movie stars, directors and screenwriters—together. Big deals. Important deals. The kind that were touted in *Variety* and talked about by envious people in the trendiest bars.

It meant, of course, working with bastards, but that didn't frighten Sushma. Partly because Holt wasn't a bastard. He was a gentleman. Handsome. Well-dressed. And, like Sushma, a UCLA grad.

Thoroughly professional. And respectful. He would make a good boss. But, mostly, Sushma knew she had right temperament.

I know how they think, because I have been a bastard, too.

She jabbed the touch screen with her thumb and listened for the ring.

ABOUT THE AUTHOR

DC Thome is the romance-writing pen name of Dave Thome, a self-employed journalist whose work has appeared in several magazines and newspapers. He's also taught writing at Marquette University and written 20 screenplays, several of which have been optioned by film production companies or won writing awards. A lifelong Wisconsin resident, he lives in the Milwaukee suburb of Shorewood with his wife of 30 years, Mary Jo.

MORE BOOKS BY DC/DAVE THOME

Man Writing a Romance by Dave Thome: A collection of humorous essays about love, sex and one man's journey into the world or romance novels. Based on the blog Man Writing a Romance, which chronicled the writing of *Palm Springs Heat*. Available for Kindle at
http://www.amazon.com/dp/B005YU8GRK

Metal Mom, A Screenplay by Dave Thome: When suburban mom Anna Petrovic shocks her husband and teenaged kids by resuming the heavy metal singing career she left behind years ago, everyone in the family needs to learn to adjust—which is more easily said than done. Available for Kindle at
http://www.amazon.com/dp/B007S6O3BG

See You In Hell by Dave Thome: A CEO killed while downsizing her company goes to hell—and takes over. She seeks revenge against the living, but slowly comes to realize who's really to blame for her unhappy life. *Available early 2013.*

Follow the Man Writing a Romance blog as DC continues Lara and Clay's story—and expands on the stories of other characters from *Palm Springs Heat* in *Fast Lane Romance #2: Malibu Bride* and *Fast Lane Romance #3: San Fernando Dreams* and to get updates on release dates.

http://manwritingaromance.blogspot.com

*Check out these popular romances by Katherine
Lowry Logan and Donna McDonald:*

The Ruby Brooch

By Katherine Lowry Logan

Prologue

Independence, Missouri, April 4, 1852

IN A SUNLIT corner of the cluttered Waldo, Hall
& Company freight office, Cullen Montgomery sat
tipped back on a chair's spindly rear legs reading the
newspaper and scratching a rough layer of morning
whiskers.

Henry Peters slumped in a leather-reading chair
and propped his legs, covered in faded cavalry pants,
on a crate marked textiles and bound for Santa Fe.
"What you learning 'bout in that gazette?"

Cullen chuckled at what little real news the paper
printed. Since he no longer lived in Edinburgh or
Cambridge, he needed to lower his expectations
when it came to the local press. Every word of the
Independence Reporter had been read and reread,
and although he couldn't find mention of a scientific

discovery or notice of a public discussion with a famous poet, he knew Grace McCoy had gotten hitched last Saturday. Reading the paper's recitation was unnecessary. He'd escorted the bride's widowed aunt to the nuptials and knew firsthand that the bride had swooned walking down the aisle. Virgin brides and widows. The former didn't interest him, the latter lavishly entertained him.

He gave the last page a final perusal. "There's no mention of our wagon train pulling out in the morning."

The old soldier took a pinch of tobacco between his thumb and forefinger and loaded the bowl of his presidential-face pipe. "We ain't got no more room anyways. No sense advertising."

The day had turned unusually warm, and Cullen had dressed for cooler weather. Sweat trickled down his back, prompting him to roll his red-flannel shirtsleeves to his elbows. "Mary Spencer's not going now. We can take on one more family."

Henry dropped his feet, and his boot heels scraped the heart-of-pine floor. "Dang. Why'd you bring up that gal's name?"

"It's not your fault she disappeared." Although Cullen hadn't said anything to his friend, he believed the portrait artist he'd seen making a nuisance of himself at the dress shop had sweet-talked the porcelain-skinned, green-eyed woman into eloping.

"Maybe, maybe not." The joints in Henry's bowed legs popped and cracked as he stood and stepped to the window.

Cullen pulled out his watch to check the time. Before slipping the timepiece back into his vest pocket, out of habit he rubbed his thumb across the Celtic knot on the front of the case. The gesture always evoked memories of his grandfather, an old Scot with a gentle side that countered his temper. Folks said Cullen walked in his grandsire's shoes. He discounted the notion he could be hotheaded, with one exception. He had no tolerance for liars. When he unveiled a lie, he unleashed the full measure of his displeasure. "We can't worry about yesterday, and today's got enough trouble of its own."

"Rumor has it John Barrett needs money. Heard you offered him a loan." Henry wagged his pipe-holding hand. "Also heard he got his bristles up, saying he wouldn't be beholdin' to nobody. Got too much pride if'n you ask me. You get down to cases with that boy and straighten his thinking out."

God knew Cullen had tried. "If I can't find a compromise, our wagon train could fall apart before we get out of town."

"You're as wise as a tree full of owls, son. You'll figure it out."

The newspaper had served its purpose, so he tossed the gossip sheet into the trash. Then he stood and stretched his legs before starting for the door.

Henry rapped his knuckles on the windowsill. "Where're you goin'?"

A queue tied with a thong at Cullen's nape reminded him that his shaggy hair hadn't seen even the blunt end of a pair of shears in months. "To the barber. Afterwards, I'll figure out how to get your wagon train to Oregon. There's a law office with my name on the door waiting at the end of the trail. I don't have time for more delays."

Henry's bushy brows merged above his nose. "There's more than work awaitin' you."

"To quote an old soldier: Maybe. Maybe not." With the picture of a San Francisco, dark-haired lass tucked into his pocket alongside his watch, and the keening sound of his favorite bagpipe tune playing in his mind, Cullen left the office to solve today's problem before it became tomorrow's trouble.

The *Ruby Brooch* can be purchased at http://www.amazon.com/The-Ruby-Brooch-ebook/dp/B007QMSONK and is available to Kindle Prime members as a free download.

Next Song I Sing

By Donna McDonald

Chapter 1

Chloe sighed heavily when she saw a magazine with ear-marked pages being pulled from the bright red overnight case tossed on the roll-a-way cot next to the window. She hung her head and groaned like a woman dying, eliciting a wicked laugh from the bag's owner.

"Emma Wallace, I can't believe you still do those silly quizzes. I will not be answering any questions about my favorite position during sex, so don't even ask."

Emma studied her friend Chloe and then pointed the magazine at her, punching the air with it for emphasis. "I'll take it easy on you because your divorce is still fresh, but you need soul-searching more than any of us, Chloe. You stayed with a man who cheated on you for more years than I did. This is not just a quiz. It's part of your journey to self-discovery."

"Journey to self-discovery? Jeez, Emma, you're starting to sound more and more like those greeting cards you write," Taylor Baird said, dragging an expensive black leather overnight case on wheels into the room behind her.

Emma and Chloe smiled at the svelte blonde who looked all business in her suit. Chloe ran over to hug her, surprised to be getting all choked up over how happy she truly was to see Taylor.

"Thank God you're here. Emma brought a *quiz*," Chloe complained, saying it as if it were a dirty word.

Finally letting Taylor go, Chloe returned to her unpacking, a little embarrassed about how incredibly happy she was to be with her friends again. God, she should never have left.

"Command some authority here, Taylor, and tell Emma no quiz questions. I moved to the West Coast to get away from being emotionally tortured," Chloe said.

Taylor laughed, her voice husky. "Remember in college when Emma got the idea that we needed to get our belly buttons pierced to be sexy?"

"Unfortunately," Chloe said, remembering the trauma all too well.

She had screamed in pain while Emma had laughed and Taylor had winced in sympathy. But ironically, Chloe had kept the piercing over the years. Mostly because it had cost her so dearly to get it, but also because it made her feel sexy even when her husband Aaron hadn't liked it. Wearing jewelry in her belly had been her way of rebelling against him when they fought, which ended up being often during the almost five years they had been married.

"Earth to Chloe? Where are you?" Emma called, waving a hand in front Chloe's face.

"That piercing hurt like hell, Em," Chloe informed her, glaring hard as she remembered the pain.

"Everything worth doing hurts a little, even exercising. And who was it that ran around in navel-revealing shirts all that year? I'll give you a hint. It wasn't me or Taylor showing off our piercings," Emma reminded her, not a bit embarrassed to gloat.

"What else could I do but show it off? I figured I might as well enjoy flaunting it after going through hell to get it done," Chloe insisted, glaring at Emma, who stuck out her tongue.

"I bet you still have your piercing," Emma said with a knowing grin. "I don't. Taylor doesn't. Tell us the truth, Chloe."

"A woman has a right to some keep some secrets, especially from nosy friends," Chloe announced, turning away from their knowing smiles.

When both Emma and Taylor both laughed, Chloe rolled her eyes because...well, she had kept her piercing. And it had felt very brave to take a healthy chunk of her savings and buy a tiny real diamond studded ring to wear there. It made her feel a lot younger than forty. She had needed help to feel better about her thirty-six-year-old husband replacing her with a skinny woman half her age.

Taylor laughed at Chloe's and Emma's bickering, thinking five years living on opposite coasts hadn't changed the dynamic between them much. Back in college though, Chloe's programming to please people she cared about had practically guaranteed she would never outsmart a determined Emma hell-bent on a make-over. Helping people improve themselves was practically a religion to Em, and she and Chloe were usually favorite converts.

"We were twenty-one not sixteen when we got those piercings, Chloe Zanders. You could have said no about the belly button ring. You can say no to the quiz now. That was my point for bringing it up. It's time to learn to command your own authority," Taylor said on a laugh.

"Trust me, Baird. I'm not the push-over I was in college. I command authority when I need to nowadays, but you're not fooling me. If I don't play along, you and Emma will think I'm just as boring as my ex did," Chloe said, turning away to shake out her clothes from the exercise duffle she had brought.

She glared at the plain black gym bag. It wasn't red and perky like Emma's or sleekly black like Taylor's. It was black and old, not to mention well-used, but her good luggage had been too large for a simple three-night stay in a resort, so Chloe hadn't bothered with it. Everything that worked for California fit in the one small bag she'd carried on the plane.

"You are so not boring, Chloe. Your ex was just a selfish jerk like my mine was. Own it, girlfriend—and then let it go," Taylor said flatly, snorting in derision. "Trust me, you didn't lose anything divorcing a man who didn't appreciate you. One day soon, you're going to be nothing but relieved Aaron is out of your life. It just takes a while to feel it."

Taylor unzipped her case and starting looking through her clothes. "Now come on. We're going shopping for sexy new dresses to kick off our weekend. For once, I'm looking forward to letting Emma try to fix me with her quizzes and questions. I haven't had a decent date in three months. I obviously need an attitude adjustment."

"It's been two weeks since my last date," Emma recounted, "but I've been sexually abstaining for several months. I'm balancing my chi and preparing for a better relationship. I want to be in an open and receptive state of being when I let the next man that far into my life."

Chloe snorted. "Balancing your chi? Wallace, you crack me up," she shook her head and sighed heavily again. "Well, don't try to balance mine, Em. I like my chi like it is. I'm still too mad at my ex to even think about sleeping with another man right now. I just want to enjoy my freedom for a while and be grateful I can stop worrying about what some guy thinks of me."

Taylor laughed, rich and full. "Well, speak for yourself. I don't even remember the last time I had sex. I think I would like someone to unbalance my chi—and soon. What I need right now though is some minor lubrication, a late lunch, and some good old fashioned girl fun."

"Taylor, I booked us appointments in the spa like you asked," Emma said, speaking to her very savvy business friend who had placed her order for the weekend with specific instructions that she would be picking up the tab for most of it. "Full works on all three of us tomorrow at ten, including massages. We're going to be buffed, fluffed, and stuffed. I hope that's what you had in mind."

"*Stuffed?* What do you mean stuffed?" Chloe demanded, gripping her most slimming black dress in her hands. "Just what kind of massages did you arrange for us, Emma? I told you I'm not ready for anything yet."

Taylor fell back on the bed laughing. "Would you listen to her? The woman who used to date three guys at once has now been replaced by an uptight version afraid of getting laid. Will you tell her sexual massages are not on the spa menu at this five star hotel? I swear I am never going to visit the east coast if Chloe is an example of what happens to people out there."

314

Emma put her chin on her chest and sighed heavily as she looked at Chloe. "I can see unwinding you is going to take some time."

"Yeah? Well, I'm about to show you two skinny blondes how much authority big women like me command. I'm going to sit on Emma's tiny butt until she tells me what she means by *stuffed*," Chloe said firmly, shaking out the five-year-old black capris that she hoped might still tame her curves.

At an extremely healthy size fourteen, Chloe was not all that big by east coast standards. But in southern California where tanned and toned bodies were the norm, she was twice the size of her two skinny friends.

"Stuffed as in lunch, Chloe. Lunch is included in our treatment." Emma demanded, shaking her head sadly. "Relax, will you? When was the last time you had any fun?"

Available for sale at your favorite ebook retailer

Check out more of Donna McDonald's work at
www.donnamcdonaldauthor.com

A FINAL NOTE ABOUT
PALM SPRINGS HEAT

*O*ne autumn day a few years ago I came down from my attic office to find my wife, Mary Jo, in her office downloading an erotic romance written by a woman she knows. Our ten-year-old freelance writing business was experiencing a lull, and she thought she could write a novella that could be published online and earning income within a few months. I thought that if she was willing to do that, I should, too. And so I started writing the book now called *Palm Springs Heat* as *Fast Lane*. As an erotic romance novella.

There were a few problems. First, writing erotic scenes cracked me up, and I thought they'd have the same effect on readers. Not the desired effect. The second was that by the time I had about half as many words as I'd need for a novella, I still had only written one sex scene. Not good for something that would be dubbed "erotic."

The choice was to try to work in more sex, or to continue writing something more traditional. I went with the latter.

Fast Lane was an old idea of mine. One of the oldest. I still have a list of twenty ideas for movie scripts

I made in the late 1980s, and *Fast Lane* is first on that list. Second on the list is *Revenge of the Everyday Housewife,* which morphed into my fifth screenplay, *Metal Mom*, which is about a woman who resumes the heavy metal singing career she gave up to raise her kids. It was optioned twice and almost became a movie a few other times. *Fast Lane*, though, I discarded after writing about five pages.

And now I'm glad I did. The *Fast Lane* I ended up with in 2011 was a lot better than the one I would have written in 1988.

I have a lot of people to thank for that. My parents, who read to me and encouraged me to write. Teachers. My editors and people I've worked with as a journalist and advertising writer.

But on *Fast Lane* in particular, I have to thank everyone who passed through the Inkslingers critique group at RedBird/RedOak in Milwaukee, especially Judy Cornfield, who set me straight on how women's clothing sizes work. Then there's Kirk Farber, Karen McQuestion and Donna McDonald, successful writers who read *Fast Lane* and gave me their unvarnished opinions about what they liked and what they didn't. Donna gets a special thanks for being one of my biggest cheerleaders and spreading the word about my blog, Man Writing a Romance, which chronicled the adventures and misadventures of writing *Fast Lane*.

I also have to thank my proofreader, Dulcie Shoener, who patiently alerted me to my over-arching problem. Literally. I must have used the words "arch" or "arched" a thousand times before she pointed them out so I could eliminate them. Connie Gage, my book cover designer, did a great job, too. I knew she'd worked with some big-timers in music, but I didn't realize how big until I Googled her *after* she finished the cover for *Fast Lane*. And all the while, she treated *me* like a star. And thanks to Dale Robert Pease of Walking Stick Books who jumped in to save my hair follicles when I was struggling with formatting the text, and who designed the cover for *Palm Springs Heat*.

The most thanks, though, goes to Mary Jo. She never did write an erotic romance, but she got a start on other projects while engineering a massive turn-around in the family business. She was also my No. 1 cheerleader. And my editor. My very tough editor. Which I needed, because every time Mary Jo marked up the margins in *Fast Lane*, it got better.

After *Fast Lane* was published, people started asking me what happens next. They thought a series was a good idea before I'd even thought of it. But then, I'd barely thought of writing even one romance novel, let alone two or three. Ideas for two more Fast Lane books started presenting themselves, so I decided to go ahead and write a series.

One of the first steps was to come up with a brand

for the series. People who know a lot about romance literature gave me some important advice: Readers like to see people on the covers and "romance" words in the titles. After brainstorming and conducting very informal focus groups, I decided to call the series the Fast Lane Romances and to rename the first book. *Palm Springs Heat.* Books two and three I named *Malibu Bride* and *San Fernando Dreams.* Each features the romantic story of a character from the first book as well as Lara and Clay's unfolding saga.

Anyway, the morals of my story are:

Write a lot.

Don't throw away any ideas.

Procrastination can be a good thing.

Get lots of feedback.

Have excellent friends.

Work with professionals.

Change can be good.

Marry an edtor.

Especially that last one. But not my editor. She's taken.

Made in the USA
Columbia, SC
20 December 2023

29114583R00195